US AGAINST EVERYBODY: A DETROIT LOVE TALE 2

MISS CANDICE

Text LEOSULLIVAN
to 22828 to join our
mailing list!

To submit a manuscript for our review,
email us at leosullivanpresents@gmail.com

US AGAINST EVERYBODY: A DETROIT LOVE
TALE 2

Previously in Us Against Everybody: A Detroit Love Tale

Life was great. If that means basically not having parents or a best friend, then yeah, life was fucking great. The only thing that made it great was the fact that Vice has constantly been in my life, despite the fact that I got into a big argument with my parents the other day. I let them know that I was seeing him regardless of the ill feelings they had towards him.

Mack – my daddy – almost made me slip up and tell my momma about his old ass being back in the drug game. I swear, I came close, but the look he gave me when I started to hint at it sent chills down my spine. I should've! What more could he do to me? He cut me off completely, and I've always been dependent of him. Not because I had to, but because that's just what I was accustomed to. He took my car and said he wasn't paying the rent at my crib anymore. I wouldn't give a fuck if the rent wasn't over a thousand dollars a month. I should've known better than to accept a house I couldn't afford on my own. A year ago, when he rented it for me, I didn't know I'd end up dealing with someone that would eventually cause him to cut me off.

Vice is taking care of everything though. That'd be great if I actually wanted him to. I felt like a burden to him. He copped me a 2015 Dodge Charger, and he paid my rent up for a year. He insisted on moving me up out of the crib, but I declined. I would've declined the car offer too, if it wasn't for me having to go back and forth to work. Speaking of work, the nigga wanted me to quit. Things were moving way too fast. Life was moving far too quickly. In a week's span, all of this had happened.

Did you notice how I said I didn't have a best friend a minute ago? Well, I didn't mean that literally. Jai and I ain't beefing or anything like that, but she's been avoiding me. She won't even talk to me. Every time I hit her up, she has an excuse to hang up – that's if she even answers the phone. Most of the time, she just shoots me a text. We've never had this problem before, and that's because before recently, Jai's never done coke. That's the only reason she was avoiding me. My boo was embarrassed, and I was trying my hardest to let her know she didn't have to be.

US AGAINST EVERYBODY: A DETROIT LOVE TALE 2

I was chilling on my patio sipping from a glass of Moscato, trying to figure out how I was going to get Jai to talk to me for more than five minutes. I missed her so much. More than anything, I wanted to get her help. According to Vice, she'd still been coping. I'm pissed the fuck off about him being her dealer. I told him to stop selling to her. He told my ass no. Vice reminded me that him not selling to her wasn't going to stop her from snorting. Cold honesty for my ass.

"What's on your mind, lil mama?" asked Vice, sliding my patio doors back closed.

"Jai. I'm going to The Crazy Horse tonight."

He sipped from my glass and nodded, "Aight, bet. I'm rolling through there with you. Niggas be on some animal shit up there at that time."

"Okay. What time is it?"

He looked down at his designer watch, "Almost ten." He frowned, "Why you drinking this weak shit? Ay, I'ma meet you there. I got some shit to take care of, beautiful."

7

I rolled my eyes and took my glass from him, "Because I like it, punk. Alright, I'm heading that way at eleven."

I told him alright like I didn't care about him leaving, but I did. He was always busy with something. The streets were talking, and although I didn't live in the hood, I knew what was up. Thanks to Facebook, I knew of all the beef going on over on Seven Mile and Riopelle.

What scared me was the fact that the problems he was having weren't only with my daddy. I knew he wasn't the most liked person in the hood, but whoever these niggas were, they were straight up gunning for Vice. In addition to dealing with beef, he was getting heat from the police. I knew fucking with a drug dealer was stressful, but I didn't know the stress would start this damn soon.

Vice kissed me on the forehead and lips before leaving.

I sighed and slipped my flip-flops on to head back in the house. I wasn't dressed. All I had on was my robe. Vice and I had just fucked in the shower and when I got out, I didn't bother putting on clothes because I didn't have plans on going anywhere. I missed my best friend though, and was going to force her ass to speak to me.

I decided to wear a simple pair of sky blue Nike yoga pants, and a fitted black t-shirt. On my feet were a pair of Nike running shoes. I wore my hair in a low ponytail. I

US AGAINST EVERYBODY: A DETROIT LOVE TALE 2

was on some laidback chill shit. I wasn't going to the club to party, so I didn't care to dress up.

My phone notification went off, and I checked it.

Carla (10:41PM): U talk 2 her?

Me (10:41PM): Nope. OMW to The Crazy Horse.

Carla (10:42PM): Come scoop me.

Me (10:42PM): Alright. Pulling up in 5.

Twenty minutes later, Vice and I were pulling up at The Crazy Horse at the same time. When he got out of the car, I saw anger written all over his face, even if he did try to mask it with a smile. When he pulled me in for a hug, I asked him what was wrong. He just smiled and told me shit was sweet. I knew he was lying. Vice introduced me to the guy he was with, as his cousin Dawson. He was visibly pissed, too.

I introduced Carla to them, and it was obvious that Dawson had taken a liking to her. Vice grabbed my hand as we walked into the club.

Gone shake that ass bitch, I'ma throw this money

9

Gone shake that ass bitch, I'ma throw this money

Gone shake that ass bitch I'ma throw this money

I'ma throw this money, I'ma throw this money.

The popular 2007 USDA hit Throw this Money was blasting from the club's speakers. On the stage was a bad ass red bone, bent over making her phat ass clap. She was killing it, and the customers were loving it. One guy was emptying a duffle bag full of money on her. Damn, I wondered if sis was getting it like that.

"What time do she go on," yelled Carla in my ear.

"I don't know. I'm about to find out," I yelled back.

Your man on the road, he doin' promo

You said, "Keep our business on the low-low"

I'm just tryna get you out the friend zone

Cause you look even better than the photos

I can't find your house, send me the info

Drivin' through the gated residential

Found out I was comin', sent your friends home

Keep on tryna hide it but your friends know

The music switched to The Weekend – The Hills, and the dancer on the stage climbed the pole to the

US AGAINST EVERYBODY: A DETROIT LOVE
TALE 2

ceiling, and seductively slid down. The way she moved reminded me of that popular stripper, Mizhani.

Vice and his boys walked in front of us. I'd occasionally peep how Dawson would lean over, say something in Vice's ear, and point to the back of the club. Even the workers in the club were whispering to each other. Every time we passed one of them, they'd whisper to their coworker. I didn't know what the fuck the talk was about. Let me check Facebook...I know somebody saying something.

I went in my bag and pulled my phone out. Before I could open my Facebook app, Carla bumped me on the shoulder to grab my attention. She pointed to the DJ booth, where we could find out what time Jai was scheduled to go on. I put my phone back in my purse and caught up with Vice and them.

"Yeah, Oozy. You remember dude?" I heard Dawson ask Vice.

Vice rubbed his chin, "Yeah, big nigga that ran with Hustle Hard..."

I interrupted them and told Vice I was about to go to the DJ booth to ask about Jai. He nodded and told me he was right behind me.

Carla and I made our way through the thick crowds and approached the DJ booth.

"Hey. What time is Barbie hitting the stage?" I yelled at him.

He bobbed his head to the music and said, "Next. Genie about to hop off."

I thanked him and left the booth.

We stood back, vibing to the music. When Genie finally left the stage, I told Carla Jai was up next. The DJ called her name over the mic, but she didn't come out. He called her a few more times, and I started to get worried. I went back up to the booth and asked him what was going on. He told me he didn't know, and then he called another dancer.

"What's wrong, brown skin?" asked Vice, noticing the frown on my face.

"Jai didn't hit the stage. I need to find her," I said.

"Aight, hold up. She fuck with Genie tough. I'ma find out what's going on. Don't worry bout it, lil' mama."

He knew I'd been bugging out about Jai's wellbeing since I caught her snorting. The club was slapping, which is why I couldn't understand why she hadn't hit the stage.

US AGAINST EVERYBODY: A DETROIT LOVE TALE 2

There was serious bread to be made, and Jai loved everything associated with making money.

"I wonder what's going on," said Carla as Vice walked in the direction of the dressing room.

Someone was near the bar causing a lot of commotion. We turned our attention over there just as the DJ cut the music.

"Ay, ay, ay! What the fuck's going on ov—"

"Somebody about to jump off the fuckin roof!" yelled some guy.

As soon as the words left his mouth, everybody went running for the exit. So many people were rushing out that the shit was like a stampede. Dawson grabbed hold of Carla and me so we wouldn't be knocked to the floor. I looked over my shoulder, trying to find Vice. As expected, he was running my way.

He grabbed hold of me, and we made our way out of the club.

"It's Barbie! What the fuck she doing up there?"

My heart dropped at the mention of Jai's stage name. Vice held me tighter.

Carla yelled, "Oh my fucking God!"

She and Dawson had made it out before us. Seeing her with her hand clasped over her mouth scared me. When we finally got outside, I looked up and there my best friend was, cup in her hand, swaying left and right.

"Y'all came to see Barbie huh," she yelled as she staggered towards the edge of the building.

"Jai…baby, please," I managed to shout over the voices of everyone else.

"Storm, bitch you came to see me too huh?" she yelled before bursting out laughing.

"Baby, please get off that ro—"

BLOCKA, BLOCKA, BOOM, BOOM, BOOM!

Shots rang out and I fell to the ground, trying to keep my eyes on Jai. I couldn't see her though. People were running, some tripping over me. I tried to stand up, but Vice pushed me back down.

"Brown skin! Stay down," he yelled as he went for the gun on his waist as shots continued to be fired.

"Is Jai o—"

US AGAINST EVERYBODY: A DETROIT LOVE
TALE 2

Before I could ask about Jai someone had answered
my question for me, "Oh my God, she's falling"

[ONE]

Vice

Pure chaos. That's all there was out to this bitch. People were running, screaming, fighting, and dying. It was crazy. All of this shit popping off while I'm trying to keep my lil' mama calm. She was losing it because her best friend was dying. With all of the commotion going on, and people laid out dodging bullets, she ended up falling on people laid out on the ground which broke her fall. What was killing Jai was the bullet she took in the chest.

"Oh my God pleeeeeease! Please," yelled Storm trying to get over to Jai who was surrounded by paramedics.

I held her as tight as I could but she was trying to get the fuck away from me.

"Let me go, Vice! Get off of me! All of this shit is your fault anyway. Those niggas were gunning for you! Now look at my best friend fighting for her fucking life!"

US AGAINST EVERYBODY: A DETROIT LOVE TALE 2

How she came at me slightly hurt a nigga but I didn't let that stop me from being there for her. She was pissed and being pissed caused her to talk stupid shit.

Yeah, those niggas were gunning for me but at the end of the day bullets ain't got no names, ya know? I wanted to cut into Storm in the worst way but I kept calm. What I should've told her was that if her stupid coke head ass friend wasn't on top of the building she wouldn't have been hit. But that'd be insensitive of me. So I shut the fuck up and held her back. But when she put hands on me, I let her crazy ass go.

"My daddy was right! I knew fucking with you was a bad idea. But fuck! I couldn't get you out of my mind. I was willing to stay with you despite the risks, but man! This shit is too real! My fucking sister is dying! Because of you! That could be me," yelled Storm.

I stood there with my arms crossed over my chest, letting her vent. I didn't say shit. Shorty was just mad because of what was going on and needed someone to blame. Of course, in a way, it is my fault but still.

She went into her in bag and handed me the car keys. I just looked at them. And when I didn't grab them she

17

dropped them on the ground and walked away. I guess that was her way of telling me it was over. But did her mad ass forget she would need that car to get back to Troy? I kneeled down and picked the car keys up.

ME (11:40PM): I put the keys in the glove box. Take care, lil' mama.

I texted her after taking the keys to her car.

I had my own problems to deal with, but instead I was being a real nigga by staying by her side. Lil' mama was just having a temper tantrum, so I'll let her have that while I handle my own shit.

I hopped behind the wheel of my whip and cranked the engine up. Dawson was sitting there loading the AK. Cuz was a fucking rider. If Reek wasn't in the 'spital he would've been sitting in the passenger seat. But cuz was a damn good replacement. He was just as nutty as me. What I liked about Reek was the fact that he was mellow, laid back. He wasn't on the same crazy shit I was on. Sometimes I needed that shit. But for times like this, I needed Dawson. I needed somebody to match my eagerness to wet a nigga shirt up.

"Where we headed cuz," asked Dawson as he sat the AK in the back.

I glanced at him, "Fuck them niggas posted at?"

US AGAINST EVERYBODY: A DETROIT LOVE TALE 2

"Who?"

I scrunched my face up, "Oozy and his squad."

Dawson shifted in his seat, "You think they behind this shit?"

"Fuck you think? Tank ain't got that kind of pull," I said as I headed in the direction of Highland Park, MI.

Tank didn't have the type of pull. The niggas that came at us were deep as fuck. Three cars to be exact. Every nigga bussin' had automatics. So like I said, Tank didn't have that type of pull. But Mack do. Still though, I'm quite sure the nigga knows Jai work there. Why would he send some niggas to shoot the place up? Plus, whoever was bussing at me saw me roll through with Storm. Mack wouldn't order a hit on me knowing his precious daughter was with me.

I could be wrong though. But after finding out Oozy's camp could be responsible for that drive-by on Riopelle a few weeks ago, I kind of figured this was him. So, Dawson could sit there on some hesitant shit all he wanted to. I knew Oozy use to post up in Highland Park when Hustle Hard was popping. So I figured he'd go right back to his old stomping grounds when he resurfaced.

What the fuck could this nigga's problem be though? I never had issues with the man. But if problems is what he wants then I don't mind. Fuck he think? They stopped making guns when they made his? Or perhaps he think just because he got clout out here I'm supposed to cur up? Fuck no. I've never been a cur type nigga in my life. A nigga's reputation don't mean a damn to me. I'm the type of cat that'll square up with Mayweather knowing he's undefeated. Fuck I look like bitching up because of what another man has done out here?

Nah, never. But I'm still confused. I've never even seen this nigga in the flesh. Never had a conversation or shit with him. So what's the issue? It's aight. I'll get down to the bottom of this shit. Hopefully bloodshed is necessary.

"You sho' you wanna go down that route," asked Dawson after lowering the volume to my radio.

I looked at him like he was crazy, "Cuz, you bitching up on me? Damn, niggas mention the name Oozy and you go soft. You the nuttiest nigga next to me, and you second guessing? All cuz the nigga gotta crazy rep?" I laughed, "Shit, I can get crazier." I pulled over on the side of the road, on Oakland and hit the brakes, "You scared cuz? Get the fuck out then. I don't have time for pussy niggas freezing up if shit gets real."

US AGAINST EVERYBODY: A DETROIT LOVE TALE 2

Dawson scrunched his face up and said, "Pull off, Vice. Don't even insult me like that, cuz. I'm just saying them niggas run d—

I yelled, "And nigga I'm a one man army! Fuck you mean they run deep? Nigga, I'm lethal by myself. I wouldn't give a fuck if a hundred niggas was coming for me. If ain't nobody riding with me, then my nigga, I'm cool with riding by myself." I paused, "So like I said, if you scared, you can get the fuck on and I'll handle this shit solo dolo, my nigga."

Dawson waved me off and said, "You know I'm riding with you, cuz. Stop talking shit."

I nodded and sped off blasting Future and Drake, Jump man.

I was serious as fuck. I would ride down alone. I couldn't give a fuck less about the recklessness. I'm reckless. I don't just talk this shit – I live it.

Ten minutes later I was pulling into the apartment complex Hustle Hard use to slang at heavy. The basketball court and parking lot was flooded with niggas. Meek Mill blasted from an old school Chevy with niggas sitting on the hood and back of it. Surrounding the car was more niggas. As soon as I pulled up next to the car, the music stopped and they approached my window.

Dawson went for the AK in the back but I stopped him.

"Nigga, these niggas ready for war! You sho you wanna do this," he asked as he frantically looked from his window to mine.

I frowned and said, "Ay cuz, get out. Walk the other way. Never in my life have I seen a nigga bitch up like this."

I took my seatbelt off and hopped out the whip.

The nigga I assume is in charge, stood in front of everyone else with his arms crossed over his muscular chest. I stood in front of him and extended my hand. Him and his niggas looked me up and down before he unfolded his arms and shook my hand.

"Wassup, Vice? Fuck you doing in HP," he asked.

See, niggas know me but I don't know who the fuck he is. Obviously he ain't the boss. Oozy is. So whoever he is, is just Oozy's flunkie. I couldn't give a fuck less about him. Who I wanted to holla at is the nigga in charge of the whole squad.

"Where Ooz at," I asked as I looked past him, over to the building.

US AGAINST EVERYBODY: A DETROIT LOVE TALE 2

"What you want with Ooz," he asked.

I chuckled and gave Dawson a hit on the arm as to say 'this nigga'.

"That's none of yo concern, young boy," I stuffed my hands in the pockets of my designer shorts, "I need to discuss boss shit with him, so as you can see my nigga...ain't yo concern."

As expected, the goons he had with him went wild. I looked at Dawson and he kept looking back at the car. Cuz wanted the chopper. We didn't need it though. Neither of us were naked out here. We had burners on us. That K would've just ate through niggas with no issue. But like I said, we didn't need it.

"Somebody looking for Oozy?"

Over all of the commotion going on, his baritone voice was heard. His niggas calmed down, and the crowd parted like the Red Sea. Oozy was respected over here, just like I was in my hood. When he came through, the crowd fell silent. His niggas kept their hands on their burners and I stood there with a smile on my face. I wish a nigga would. I prayed a nigga would try.

23

Oozy stood in front of who he had in charge.

I looked up at him and nodded, "We need to rap about some shit."

I hated looking up to niggas. I'm a tall nigga, but Oozy is giant tall. Nigga gotta be around seven feet. He looked down at me, nodded and told me to follow him. When he peeped Dawson following us he said just me. I respected that and told cuz to kick back in the whip. Ain't like the nigga really wanted to be there anyway. He nodded and told me to holla if he needed me.

I followed Oozy into the building and we went up the stairs to the second floor. He unlocked the door, and ducked as he went in. I followed him in and took a seat on the cheap microfiber couch. He sat across from me on a loveseat and lit a blunt.

He took two pulls from it and passed it to me. I leaned over and took a couple pulls from it before passing it back to him.

"What you wanna rap about," he finally asked.

"You got some type of issue with me?"

He frowned up and said, "Fuck is you talking about? I don't even know you, lil' fella." He took a pull from the blunt and blew a thick cloud of smoke out, "I got respect for you because I know who you are. That's the only reason we sitting in this mothafucka chopping it up."

US AGAINST EVERYBODY: A DETROIT LOVE TALE 2

I was confused, "So you ain't gunning for me?"

Oozy laughed, "Now why would I do that? Shit's sweet over here, my dude. No need to start unnecessary beef." He shook his head, "Nah, I'm getting too old for that shit. I had enough back in the day."

I sat back on the couch after he passed me the blunt and said, "Damn. I just knew it was you."

He shook his head, "Nah not me." Oozy sat up, "I'ma tell you like this though my dude, most of the time the beef ain't even from the outside. It's the niggas you closest to. And I'm speaking from experience. Keep yo eyes open, and yo finger on the trigger at all times, my nigga."

I took a pull from the blunt and let what he said marinate. Could it be my nigga though? Naaaah. Bro took a bullet. Reek wouldn't snake a nigga. Would he? Immediately, I grew paranoid. I took two more pulls from the blunt, sat up, and passed it back to Oozy.

I stood up, and he did too.

I gave him some dap and said, "Good looking out, OG."

Oozy nodded, "Ain't no thang."

I left the apartment with a lot to think about.

Reek's been riding with a nigga since day one. He got money, like I got money. So what could be his issue though? Man, nah, my nigga ain't a fuck nigga. It ain't him. Loyalty is rare, and that nigga Reek loyal as fuck. Besides, he know exactly how the fuck I gets down. I might let him slide every now and then but bro ain't stupid enough to snake me like this. I won't hesitate to send him straight to his maker.

I left the building and headed to my whip, with niggas giving me all types of looks. You know me, I wore a smile on my face. These type of niggas are trigger happy and wanted some shit to pop off. But nah, when bosses link up boss shit pops off. There's no need for gun play if mutual respect is established.

Just as I was about to jump in the whip, something came to me. I swear I just peeped a familiar face in the crowd of niggas. I let the door handle go, and Dawson hopped out the whip. He asked me if everything was straight. I waved him off and approached the crowd of niggas who still had their hands on their burners.

I squinted my eyes as I narrowed in on the faces.

"Fuck is you doing," asked the nigga from earlier.

US AGAINST EVERYBODY: A DETROIT LOVE TALE 2

I ignored and pushed him aside. I was looking for the shit I peeped a minute ago. If I saw who the fuck I think I saw, I'm acting a fucking donkey.

Well, I'd be damned.

The nigga tried to inch his way back into the building but I caught up with him before he could. I snatched him back by his shirt and he went falling backwards, onto the ground. Fuck nigga fell so hard, his head coming in contact with the ground made a loud thud noise. I knew his shit was split wide open. It was dark out, but the street light shining on us showed me the small puddle of blood underneath his head.

"Fuck you doing over here," I yelled as I kneeled down next to him.

"Man, Vice, let me ex—

"Ay, it don't even matter, my nigga," I said, interrupting whatever weak ass lie Darnell was about to spill out of his mouth.

I pulled my burner out and touched his forehead with him.

27

"What's popping, cuz," asked Dawson as he kneeled down and touched D with his burner, too.

"Disloyalty at an all-time high out to this mothafucka," I yelled into Darnell's ear.

I didn't know what the fuck the nigga was doing over in HP, when he was supposed to be making sure shit was moving smooth over on Riopelle. I didn't give a fuck enough neither. My paranoia told me he was snaking a nigga. And with how the way shit's been going on, everybody on some sus shit was going to get this work.

"Man, come get this nigga! I didn't do shit," yelled Darnell just as Oozy walked out of the building.

"Aye, my mans," said Oozy, with his head down as he scrolled through his phone.

I cocked my head to the side and said, "What nigga?!"

"This right here is my territory. I don't get down like that. And when you in my hood, neither will you." He put his phone in his pocket, "I don't give a fuck about what the nigga did to piss you off."

I turned my attention back to the crying nigga beneath me. I cocked my gun back, ready to send a hot one to his memories. But before I could pull the trigger, Dawson grabbed my arm snapping me back to reality.

"We can't off this nigga out in the opening like thi—

US AGAINST EVERYBODY: A DETROIT LOVE TALE 2

"Nigga why not," I yelled, cutting him off.

Dawson inched in closer to me, "Cause nigga…this ain't the six or the seven! We don't know these fuck niggas out chea!" He bit down on his bottom lip, "They don't owe you loyalty or respect. Shit, could be a snitch nigga in the crowd cuz!" he glanced up at Oozy, "And this ain't a nigga we want beef with, feel me?"

I couldn't give a fuck less about beefing with Ooz. What I gave a fuck about was the point he made about us not being in our hood. He was right; one of these niggas could possibly snitch on me. And I couldn't have that. I'd have to shed blood all over HP.

I turned the burner away from Darnell, and snatched him up by his collar.

"You know this nigga," I asked Oozy as I pushed Darnell's face closer to him.

Oozy squinted his cocked eyes before saying, "Lil' weak ass nigga always begging to be down with the squad. Who is he?"

"Nobody. You can call him deceased though," I said before walking away.

US AGAINST EVERYBODY: A DETROIT LOVE
TALE 2

[TWO]
Storm

I was a nervous wreck. My leg bounced as I sat there
biting at my coffin nails. Sitting in the waiting room of
Receiving Hospital waiting to get news on Jai's condition
was killing me. I felt responsible for everything. If I
would've been a better friend she would've been well. I
should've gotten her help as soon as I found out about her
new habit. But shit, she wouldn't accept my calls. I
should've been better. I should've popped up on her ass a
long time ago. I was so wrapped up in Vice that I was
neglecting my friend. I felt like shit. I've always been
there for Jai. Now when she needed me most, I left her
hanging.

Although I wasn't waiting alone, I felt alone. I was
sitting here in the waiting room with my parents, not

saying a got damn word to them. They were here because we're all Jai got. Carla left an hour ago, and I wish she could've stayed. The tension was thick as hell. When they got here, they hugged me and wiped my tears away but I got up and moved. I wasn't fucking with them like that. They disrespected the hell out of me the last time we were together. Said I didn't really mean anything to Vice. Mack even went as far as saying I was just one of Vice's ho's of the month. Called me stupid and everything. So, fuck them.

I felt bad, treating my momma this way because we had a great relationship. It was breaking my heart. I felt her staring at me but I didn't even lift my head to look her way. When I heard footsteps approaching me, I knew she was coming my way. I stood up, grabbed Jai's belonging bag, and walked in the other direction.

And then, Mack opened his disrespectful mouth.

"Fuck her, Tati. She got her head so far up Vice's ass that she don't realize that this happened because of him. She'll be running back to us when he's finished with her young ripe ass."

I whipped my head around so fast that I smacked myself in the face with my hair, "Just so you know, ma, he's back in the game with his old, played out ass."

Just as I expected, he came after me. I took off running before he could even get up from his seat. Before I made it to the restroom, I looked over my shoulder and

US AGAINST EVERYBODY: A DETROIT LOVE TALE 2

my momma held him. My daddy was pissed at me, but I honestly don't think he would hurt me. He probably was going to try to shake some sense into me. Whatever the case, I didn't want him to put his hands on me period so I stayed in the restroom. I needed to get back to the waiting room, though. I needed to be there when they updated us regarding Jai's condition.

I leaned over the sink with my head down. Why did Mack have to start with me? I'm already feeling fucked up as is. And for him to mention Vice really put me in a bad head space.

When I left them car keys on the ground, I intended on leaving my feelings there as well. What the fuck was I thinking? I've had my share of heart break to know that it just isn't that easy. Especially when it comes to a nigga like Vice. It broke my heart all over again when my daddy said his name and told me exactly what I already knew – that Vice was responsible. I hated to have to end things with him. But I had to, right? That could be me laid up on that operating table. I could've been the one hit. And who's to say it wouldn't happen next time? I did tell him I was rocking with him regardless of the risks. But shit, I didn't think about how real shit could get.

I'm not cut out for that life. Hell no! I've never dealt with a man anything like Vice. So for me to be okay with niggas riding through, shooting shit up is pretty far-fetched. I thought I was about that life – obviously not. I was scared shitless.

There was a knock on the door. I didn't say anything and whoever it was tried to come in.

"Storm." It was momma.

I sighed and unlocked the door. She came in with a wet face and puffy red eyes. I've never seen my beautiful momma look so distraught in my life.

Tatianna – my mom – is a brown skin, curvy woman. She has an exotic look about her. 5'5 with slanted brown eyes, and full lips. Just like me, except I'm a lot shorter and slim.

She closed the door behind her and just stood there.

"What ma," I asked, trying my best not to sound rude.

She threw her hands up, "My family is falling apart!" she chuckled as tears fell from her eyes, "Hell, the divorce wasn't even this stressful. My daughter is in love with a drug deal—

"You and Mack love calling the pot black! Ma, don't even go the—

US AGAINST EVERYBODY: A DETROIT LOVE TALE 2

She stepped to me and pointed her finger in my face, "Shut the hell up, Storm, and let me finish! Your dad might not put hands on you, but trust me, I will!" I rolled my eyes and she continued, "You might be grown, but if you roll your eyes again I'ma knock them out of your head!"

My momma and I might have a 'sister girl' relationship but she knew when to turn it off. When she's mad and in mommy mode, she's scary as fuck so I simmered down and apologized.

"Like I was saying…everything is falling apart and the common factor in all of this mess is Vice." She shook her head, "He must be something special to have you go against your family and to have you risk your li—

I cut her off, "I broke up with him, aight?!"

"Stop interrupting me, Storm! Do it again, I'm knocking your teeth straight down your throat," she threatened with her finger in my face, "Now a young woman I consider my daughter is laid up in the hospital with a bullet in her chest, strung out on coke. And again, Vice is the reason for it."

"Vice is not the reason Jai is on coke! She formed that habit on her own! So, please, stop blaming Vice for everything. And he is not the reason things are falling apart between us. Everything is falling apart because my parents won't let me live and love who I want to love!"

Did I really just admit to loving him? Why am I even defending him? I really just couldn't stand there and let her blame him for everything when that's not even the case. The only thing he's partially responsible for is Jai getting shot.

Knock! Knock!

"The doctor's out here," yelled my daddy.

"Is he calm," I asked my ma.

"Calm or not, you know he'll never hurt you."

Before we walked out of the restroom, I stopped her and gave her a hug. I apologized as well, in return she told me she might not like the lifestyle Vice lives but she supports me if it's him that I choose to love. I sadly told her that none of that even mattered anymore because I broke up with him. It doesn't matter if I love him. If I stay with him, my life will always be in danger.

"Ms. Ford is stabilized and in recovery. She'll be transferred to the trauma unit in a few hours. I suggest you all to go home and rest up, seeing as though she might not be up for visitation for a while. In addition to her gunshot wound, Ms. Ford suffers from broken bones

US AGAINST EVERYBODY: A DETROIT LOVE
TALE 2

as a result of her fall. She's in pretty bad shape, but she'll make it," said Dr. Kelsey as we sat in the family waiting area.

"Can I go see her now? I need to see her," I pleaded, totally ignoring what he just told us.

My ma rubbed my back, "Not right now sweetie. You had a stressful night. Go home and get some sleep, Storm. We've been here all night."

She was right. I needed rest. It was after five in the morning. We've been here waiting for over four hours. I'm hungry and exhausted but I need to see her.

"But…"

"But nothing," said Mack, with an attitude, interrupting me, "Come back later Storm."

The doctor excused himself and Mack continued, "Me? I'm about to hit the block!"

I didn't have the energy to respond to the subliminal threat he just made against Vice.

"Derek, you're taking your old ass home! You don't have any business 'hitting the block', what the hell," yelled my ma calling my dad by his government name.

His jaw clinched; he hated being called Derek.

"Mind yo business, Tati!"

I had enough and would rather be in bed, than sitting around listening to them argue. I told them I was going home. Mama wanted me to go home with her but I declined. I just wanted to be left alone. I hugged and told her I loved her before I departed.

I didn't say a word to my dad.

*

As soon as I hit the door, I stripped my clothes off and headed to the bathroom to shower. I was sleepy as hell but there was no way in hell I was about to jump straight into bed with dried up blood on me.

I turned the shower on, adjusted the water to my preference, and then stepped inside. I grabbed my bath sponge and lathered my body with Bath and Body Works shower gel. I closed my eyes as the warm body cascaded over my body. Tears fell from my eyes as last night's events played through my mind like a movie. It was like a horror film. So many people were injured. Screaming. Gun fire. It was so chaotic. I had never been involved in

US AGAINST EVERYBODY: A DETROIT LOVE TALE 2

anything so traumatic in my life. And to think, that was the norm for Vice.

As I cleaned my 'woman part', Vice ran through my mind. Falling in love with him was inevitable. He was like a drug. He was my bad habit. As much as things needed to be over between us, I couldn't help but yearn for him. His touch. To hear his voice. Hell, a simple text would suffice.

Although I dumped him, he could've at least called or texted to check up on me. As quickly as that though entered my mind, I dismissed it. I was being selfish. Vice was probably out trying to track down whoever was responsible for the drive by. Thinking of him out on the streets on some wild shit sent a chill of terror through my body. Oh God! I pray to God he's okay. See, this type of shit is just too stressful to deal with.

I rinsed off and got out of the shower. As I dried off, I thought I should text to see if he was okay. I stared at my phone sitting on the sink and decided against it.

After locking up, and throwing me and Jai's clothes in the washing machine, I headed for bed. I turned the light on and damn near had a heart attack.

Vice was lying in my bed in his boxers, lightly snoring. As much as I wanted to wake him and curse him out I just turned the light out and climbed into bed. I lied as far away from him as possible. But, in his sleep, he found me and pulled me closer.

With his face buried in my neck, and arms wrapped around my waist he said, "I love you, lil' mama."

*

I rolled over and grabbed my phone from the nightstand. It was after one in the afternoon. My drapes had been open, and Vice was no longer lying next to me. I lied on my back with the biggest smile on my face. He told me he loved me. I know he was sleep but that doesn't mean didn't mean it. Although being with him is out of the question, I'm still giddy as hell about him confessing his love for me.

I clicked on his contact icon and selected the text messaging option.

ME (1:12PM): So you just leave without saying good-bye?

I yawned and slipped on my house shoes before starting my day. I needed to get down to the hospital pronto. But first, I had to inform Ryan of what happened

US AGAINST EVERYBODY: A DETROIT LOVE
TALE 2

and get rid of the coke I found stashed in the pockets of
Jai's clothes. She had a little under an eight ball worth.
The shit hurt me to the core. Jai's really on that shit. It's
so hard to digest. She has to get help.

Anyway, I know Ryan's been trying to reach Jai like
crazy. The only thing I hated about reaching out to him,
was that I'd have to get his number from B to do so. I
couldn't stand his ass now. He possessed every quality of
a fuck nigga.

I was ass naked, and a little chilly so I grabbed my
robe before heading to the kitchen. I needed some coffee.
Although I got a little rest in, I was still very tired. I
scratched my head and yawned as I walked into the
kitchen.

"I know yo breath smelling 'bout foul as fuck right
now."

I jumped out of surprise and clenched my chest,
"Vice! What are you doing here?"

He was standing at my stove, scrambling eggs,
"Cooking breakfast for lunch. You glad a nigga didn't
leave without saying good-bye right?"

41

I narrowed my eyes at him, "You're not supposed to be here period." I walked over to my Keurig and started it up, "To be real, home boy."

He waved me off, "Pass me the pancakes out the microwave, brown skin."

I opened the microwave and handed him the plate of blueberry pancakes, "Don't ignore me, Vice."

He finally stopped scrambling the eggs and turned to me. He sat the spatula down and approached me. Vice stared into my eyes before kissing me on the lips. I covered my mouth and told him I hadn't brushed.

"I dig you, lil' mama, funky breath and all."

I smirked, "Dig me? Or love me?"

He was back at the stove, putting the eggs on the plate, "Fuck is you takin' bout?"

I giggled and poured my coffee before sitting on a barstool, "Nothing. Like I said, you're not supposed to be here."

"I'm exactly where I'm supposed to be," he sat a plate of sausages, pancakes, and eggs in front of me. "Stop bugging."

Vice sat across the table from me and took a sip of my coffee before asking, "Jai straight?"

US AGAINST EVERYBODY: A DETROIT LOVE
TALE 2

I shifted in my seat, "She good. Vice, are we going
to discuss the elephant in the room?"

"Shit got wild as fuck last night. I apologize about
that lil' mama. I promise, I'll do whatever necessary to
make sure it never happens again."

He was beating around the bush, like saying he'll
make sure it'll never happen again would fix everything.
It wouldn't. I dug into my eggs and closed my eyes as the
cheesy goodness hit my taste buds. Usual, I'm skeptical
about eating other people's eggs, but his were damn
good.

"What you put in these eggs?"

He took a bit of his sausage and said, "Nacho cheese,
salt and pepper, and parsley."

I nodded and finished them off before moving on to
the other food.

"You don't strike me as the type of man to cook."

"I don't cook. I haven't cooked in years. Consider
yourself special, lil mama."

I decided that it'd be best to switch the subject from last night. I could tell he didn't want to talk about it and since I was enjoying his company I put a pause on it. But trust, I will be revisiting it. I don't need him thinking I've just swept it under the rug. Because I haven't. It'd be impossible.

We sat and talked for a good thirty minutes like everything was fine. I can't lie and say Vice doesn't make me happy. He makes me very happy. Talking with him was the perfect distraction I needed. Had I been alone, my thoughts would've been sad. I would've been stressing about Jai. But not with Vice. With Vice I laughed and smiled like I didn't have a care in the world. As I sat and talked with him 'what ifs' clouded my mind. What if I stayed with him? Could it be so bad? He said he'll always protect me. What if? Falling in love with him was kismet. We're destined to be together, right? Isn't that why God placed the perfect man in my life? What if I did sweep the incident under the rug? Would it be so bad?

I stared into his hazel eyes as I downed the rest of my coffee, "I'm happy you're here, Vice."

He smiled, "I'm happy I'm here too, brown skin." He finished off his juice, "That fuck shit you was on last night is deaded right?"

He was referring to my subliminal break up. I was speechless though. Because no matter how drawn I was to him. Nor how happy he made me. The fact still

US AGAINST EVERYBODY: A DETROIT LOVE TALE 2

remained; Vice is a dangerous person. But shit, can't we be in danger together? Am I really considering risking my life to be with a man? A damn good man, might I add. The hood ass nigga cooked me breakfast. Where they do that at?

"Let me think on it, Vice."

He stood up and carried our plates to the sink, "Aight, you can think on it. Last night was crazy as fuck. So yeah, think on it. I'ma catch up with you later. You should have your decision by then."

"Where you about to go," I asked with an attitude I tried my best to hide.

I didn't want him to leave. We were having a good time. Such a good time that I had forgotten all about my plans to visit Jai as soon as I woke up.

"I got some shit to take care of. Reek getting out of the hospital too, so I gotta scoop bro up," he walked around the table and kissed me on the forehead, "I hope you make the right decision Storm. I'd hate to have to live in this cold world without you."

We stared into each other's eyes as he spoke. In the eyes of a thugged out, killer, I saw love. Vice loved me. His reaction to me bringing it up earlier was defensive so I'm sure he doesn't remember uttering those three words. It's fine though, because I have all of the confirmation I need.

"I wish things could be different," I replied as sadness came over me.

He rubbed my face and said, "Like I wasn't involved in this street life. Shit, shorty, I wish that too. Losing you wouldn't even be an option." He smiled, "Despite that though, lil mama, you'll be mine. I told you; you were made for me. Can't change destiny."

I laughed, "You sure you don't remember what you said?"

He winked at me before walking away, "I remember. Just tell a nigga you love him too."

I smiled, "I love you too, Vice."

US AGAINST EVERYBODY: A DETROIT LOVE
TALE 2

[THREE]

Jai

I woke up in an excruciating amount of pain. It took me a minute to become aware of my surroundings. I couldn't remember why I was in the hospital nor anything from the night before. So when I woke up barely able to move, I went crazy. Well, as crazy as my pain would allow me to. I was confused. I had a cast on my arm and bandages all over my body.

I grabbed the call light and pushed it repeatedly. I needed answers and for the life of me I couldn't understand why I didn't remember shit.

The door opened and instead of a nurse walking in, like I expected, it was Genie.

"What the fuck you doing here?!"

She looked over her shoulder as she approached my bed, "I'm just here to make sure you don't run your mouth about what happened last night."

"Bitch, I don't even know what happened, so how am I going to run my mouth?" I winched in pain as I tried to make myself comfortable, "What are you talking about?"

Genie shook her head, "Mention my name and bitch, you'll wish that bullet would've killed yo ass."

I wanted to hop my injured ass right out of bed and onto her. She had me fucked up. I wanted to beat her ass so bad, that I had tears running down my face. I was super pissed about not being able to put hands on her. And how she's just standing there gawking down at me, threatening me and shit told me she was responsible for this shit.

"What did you do to me bitch," I yelled as I tried to get out of bed.

Genie laughed and backed up, "Nothing you didn't want me to do. Ain't nobody tell yo stupid ass to bite off more than you could chew," she shook her head, "Rookie, lightweight ass bitch." she walked away and then looked over her shoulder, "Oh, and Julien said you're fired."

MISS CANDICE

US AGAINST EVERYBODY: A DETROIT LOVE TALE 2

I couldn't give a fuck less about being fired. I could easily shake my ass at Erotic City. Hell, they had more clientele any-fucking-way and would be glad to get a bad bitch like me. Still, the last thing on my mind was twerking for a few dollars.

Genie walked out of the room and I tried my hardest to remember last night. But everything was blur. I really couldn't remember and that bothered me. What the fuck did Genie give me? I ran my hand over my face and sighed. Life for me has never been this stressful. Ever since I started dancing at The Crazy Horse shit ain't been nothing but bad.

And to top it off, I'm nauseated. I needed some coke. My stomach was hurting. My body was begging for that white potent powder. I frantically darted my eyes from one side of the hospital room to the other. My shit wasn't here. I needed to take the edge off. What the hell is wrong with me? Even if my belongings were here, the coke sure in the fuck wouldn't be. I sighed a sigh of relief. My things weren't here so that meant my coke was safe. Safe where though?

I hit the call button again. I swear to God I can't stand hospitals. How are you going to be working in a hospital but too busy to be there when someone calls? Bitch, I could be dying!

A young, dark skin girl walked into the room in burgundy scrubs. Off top, I knew she had an attitude. I could tell it was busy because of the heavy traffic outside of my room.

"Can I help you," she asked with an attitude as she stood next to my bed with her hands on her hips.

I shook my head, "Yes you can. I don't know what happened to me."

She sighed and said, "You were shot. Do you need anything else?"

I giggled and took notice to her nametag that read 'Brittany', "Bitch, you lucky I can't get up out of this bed! I swear on my daddy I'd put these hands on you! Just send my nurse in, because obviously you ain't her. It's not my fault you're overworked and underpaid."

She started to say something but I shot her a look that made her ass get out. Since I couldn't put hands on her, I planned on hitting her where it hurt most – her pockets. Yeah, I couldn't wait to leave a nasty review about Brittany and how she treated me during my stay. I might be a petty bitch, but like I said I'm only doing it because I couldn't whoop her black ass.

US AGAINST EVERYBODY: A DETROIT LOVE TALE 2

I was full of frustration and she couldn't be professional nor compassionate enough to realize that. I just needed to know how I ended up in the hospital. *I was shot...* but by who? What in the fuck did I get myself into? Sometimes I can be a wild bitch but I don't have beef with anybody. Hell, the way Genie's ho ass was just talking, seemed like she's the one who shot me.

Five minutes later the door opened again and a tall, slender white woman in light blue walked in smiling. She had to be my nurse. I appreciated the reassuring smile. Unlike Brittany, she really cared.

She stood at my bed and extended her hand, "Good Afternoon Ms. Ford. I'm your nurse, Kelly. I understand you have a few questions. I'm sure you do! Waking up in the hospital is scary." She walked away and pulled a chair over, "How are you feeling?"

"Call me Jai. And I'm in a lot of pain. I don't remember what happened to me," I told her as my eyes drifted off into space.

She sighed, "That's understandable, considering the fact that your blood alcohol level was fatally high." She cleared her throat, "And a variety of drugs were found in your system. But before we get to that, let me just fill you in."

"Wait…A variety of drugs? What the fuck you mean? All I do is smoke weed…and…" I paused, "Snort coke occasionally."

Kelly nodded, "Okay. But we also found a high dosage of Xanax, and um… Molly."

I instantly sat straight up despite being in pain.

"What the fuck?!"

"Jai, please calm down sweetie. Let me fill you in. Please."

"I don't do anything but weed and coke! What the fuck you mean!?"

I was heated. I couldn't stop the tears from falling from my eyes no matter how much I tried. I was hurt! Damn hurt. I'm fucking Genie up, and that's on my mothafucking life! That bitch did this! She was jealous because my bad ass was on the come up. Ain't no way in hell I willingly did that shit. The fuck I look like doing molly?! Come on now! That's not me! But then again, snorting lines ain't me neither. Still, though! I didn't do that shit.

Nurse Kelly reached over and grabbed my trembling hand, "Listen, Jai, I know this is all hard to digest. And

US AGAINST EVERYBODY: A DETROIT LOVE TALE 2

we can talk more about that in a second. What I want to talk to you about now is –

For the first time since I opened my eyes, I noticed a young girl sitting on the other side of the room in a pair of scrubs reading a book.

"And who the fuck is that?!"

"Shhh. Relax honey. Iesha is just here sitting with you to make sure you don't hurt yourself. Y—

"Why in the hell would I hurt myself?!"

I was going crazy. I kept trying to snatch my hand away from Kelly but the grip she had on my hand was firm.

"Please let me explain. When you were shot, you were standing on top of The Crazy Horse. Since you've been unconscious we assumed you were making a suicide attempt."

I calmed down. My body fell limp as I leaned back onto the pillows. What have my life become? My daddy is turning over in his grave right now. He was such a hardworking, put-together man that I should've followed

53

in his footsteps. Instead I let how hard he worked spoil me. I looked to men to give me the same financial security my dad did. I was taking the pussy way out.

I'm saying all of this now, but in the back of my mind I know I won't do better. After I'm discharged and well enough, I'll be taking my ass right down to Erotic City to see about a job. Maybe I should be a waitress. Them bitches get bread too. I can't lie and say the fast money of dancing didn't make me spoiled. In a way, I'm still looking at men for financial security but at least I'm actually working for it now.

"Jai, are you okay?"

"I wasn't trying to kill myself. She can go. I don't need a fucking babysitter, aight?" I rolled my eyes and looked around the room for my belongings bag like I didn't already realize my things weren't here. I was losing my got damn mind.

"Where are my things?"

"A young woman by the name of Storm thought it'd be best if she took your things home with her."

I rolled my eyes. Great. I know that bitch went through my shit and threw my coke away. Yeah, I called her a bitch and I meant it. Where is she? She's not here with me. Storm knows her and her people are the only family I have. How come she's not here in my time of need?

US AGAINST EVERYBODY: A DETROIT LOVE TALE 2

I turned my head in the direction the sitter was sitting in and said, "I told you to go! I don't need anybody sitting around watching my every move. I can't do shit! How in the hell am I going to hurt myself in the fucking hospital."

I'm feigning – bad! No one is safe from my wrath. The girl flinched and closed her book. She looked to Nurse Kelly for reassurance. Kelly just nodded her head and told the girl to wait for her at the nurses' station. The young girl wished me well, and walked out.

I closed my eyes and tried to think of something other than needing my coke. I needed it bad. I was so nauseous. And every time I gagged, my ribs contracted causing pain. I sat up and placed my hand over my stomach. The pain was excruciating.

"Jai, how do you rate your pain," asked Kelly who was now standing at a laptop on wheels.

"10. I need something for nauseous and the strongest pain meds you got in this bitch."

"Why you in here being so damn mean?!"

I looked past Kelly at Storm who was walking in with balloons and a teddy bear. I sat back on the pillows and rolled my eyes. Storm walked over to the bed and kissed me on the cheek. I turned my nose up at her. I was being a real bitch. Okay, so what she didn't stay the night? What should matter is the fact that she's here now.

"Ugh, why you being funky with me," asked Storm, sitting a gift bag in my lap.

"Did you bring my stuff?"

She gave me the side-eye, "Nah. I have your phone though." She handed me my phone and I sat it on my food table. "I'll stop at your place and bring you clothes and stuff when you're discharged."

Nurse Kelly excused herself and told me she would bring me meds.

I shook my head, "Storm, I need my stuff."

She ignored me and said, "I'm so happy you're here sis. I swear, if I would've lost you I would've lost my mind." She sat in the same chair Nurse Kelly was once sitting in, "Man, last night was crazy as hell."

"You were there?"

Her eyes were full of worry as her perfectly arched eyebrows knitted together, "What you mean? You know I was there. You don't remember?"

"No," I said before embarrassingly looking away.

US AGAINST EVERYBODY: A DETROIT LOVE
TALE 2

"Oh, Jai," said Storm, her tone dripping with
sadness.

I wiped a tear from my eyes, "Sis...I'm...shit is
bad."

Storm stood up and leaned over the railing to hug
me. She rubbed my back as she ran down everything that
happened. I, in return, told her everything Kelly told me.
I still can't believe all of that shit was found in my
system. How could I go from only smoking weed to
doing all this extra shit? It's the stripper life I've grown
addicted to. As much as I hated to admit it, I was self-
destructing. And not doing a damn thing about it. Just
like I said, I'm taking my dumb ass right down to Erotic
City when this is over.

"Who them niggas have beef with," I asked Storm
after she finished telling me anything.

She walked away from the bed and said,
"Umm...they were shooting at Vice."

I giggled, "And you was worried about catching a
bullet fucking with that nigga." I shook my head and

looked up to the ceiling, "You're not beating him up because of this shit, right, bitch?"

Shock filled her eyes, "What? Of course. What the hell you mean? I'm not fucking with him. Look at you Jai! You laid up because of him!"

"Let be real. I'm laid up in here because, unlike the other mothafuckas outside of the club, I was on top of a building. I didn't duck for cover and just like you know, bullets ain't got no names! That ain't his fault, sis. Do not trip on him."

"Well, I don't care about what you rapping about. Fucking with that nigga is risky."

I winched in pain, "Ahh…shit!" I frowned my face up and tried to lie on my side, "You knew it was risky when you agreed to be with him. Don't bitch up now, sis. Besides, like I said, Vice won't let anything bad happen to you. What happened last night was my fault. Not his."

Storm looked at me with so much worry written on her face, "Jai…I hate seeing you like this. Please promise me you'll get help." Tears rolled down her cheeks, "I don't care to talk about Vice, to be honest. I want to talk about you. I need you out here Jai." She walked over to the side of my bed, "I almost lost my mind last night. I can't fathom living in a world without my best bitch in the whole world."

US AGAINST EVERYBODY: A DETROIT LOVE TALE 2

I didn't promise her anything. Instead, I mustered up a smile and reached out for a hug. When she hugged me she told me she talked to Ryan and that he'd be up here shortly. I didn't want to see him but I knew I had to. I couldn't shut him out right now. No matter how much I'm feigning for a hit, I won't let that get in the way of getting my rent paid next month.

[FOUR]

Vice

Niggas were comfortable because I let them be. I shouldn't have. That's where I fucked up. One thing I hated more than anything was disloyalty. What I failed to realize is that there is no loyalty in the dope game. Not even from the nigga you call your right hand and definitely not from family. All that loyalty shit goes out of the window as soon as money is involved. Fuck, it don't matter how much you look out for a nigga they always want more. Greed. If it's not what the boss nigga is making, it's never enough. Greed is what makes niggas make dumb decisions.

I'm sitting in front of Reek's crib, breaking a swisher down, blasting *What a Time to Be alive*. Bro got out of the hospital three days ago. He didn't know I was out here. It was after two in the morning. I couldn't sleep. My mind wouldn't stop racing. I felt like somebody was really out to get me. Darnell was a disloyal mothafucka but he ain't got enough pull to orchestrate the shit that has been going on in my life. Drama and gun play was at an all-time high. Even in his absence so I knew the shit

US AGAINST EVERYBODY: A DETROIT LOVE
TALE 2

was coming from a different angle. And like Ooz said, it's usually the nigga closest to you.

I sprinkled the kush in the blunt and rolled it up, with my eyes on Reek's house. I watched several lights come on and go off. The beat woke him up. Not only him but the neighbor was standing in the door but the bitch didn't have guts enough to tell me to lower my music. She opened the screen door and turned her nose up. So you know what I did? I turned the stereo up to the max. She rolled her eyes and slammed the door. Bitch.

Reek stood in his door. I turned my bright lights on and he shielded and squinted his eyes. I stuck my head out of the window and said, "What up, fuck nigga?!"

"Vice? Bro, what the fuck you doing out here," asked Reek blocking the beaming light from his eyes.

"Rolling a fatty. Come blow one with cha boy," I said as I turned my bright lights off.

He looked over his shoulder and said, "Nigga, I'm about to get my dick wet."

I lowered my music and yelled, "Fuck that rat ass bitch Keesh."

"How you kn—

"Cause you's a stupid nigga cuffing the loosest bitch on the six," I shook my head, "I said come blow with cha boy!"

Reek sucked his teeth but he peeped the seriousness in my tone of voice. I wasn't playing with the nigga. He told me to hold up and I nodded then turned my stereo back up. I reclined my seat and lit the blunt. As I looked at the fiery red tip, I thought of shoving it in Reek's eye. But on the other hand, I was still struggling with actually believing Reek was capable of being a snake. Like I said, he took a fuckin bullet.

In addition to that, I didn't get that vibe. Reek could be a little stupid with the decisions he made at times, but I didn't feel as if he was disloyal. I move off impulse. And my gut ain't telling me he's the snake. I was still going to fuck with him just because.

I needed to pick his brain. Maybe I was letting the history me and the nigga had cloud my judgement. But on the real, don't think for a second that I won't blow the niggas brains all over my interior if need be. Fuck you thought? I don't tolerate snakes. I'll rip the skin off that niggas face.

US AGAINST EVERYBODY: A DETROIT LOVE TALE 2

I took a pull from the blunt and closed my eyes, vibing to the music.

Jumpman, Jumpman, I don't need no introduction

Jumpman, Jumpman, Metro Boomin on production, wow

Hundred cousins out in Memphis they so country, wow

Tell her stay the night, valet your car, come fuck me now

Jumpman, Jumpman, live on TNT I'm flexing

Jumpman, Jumpman they gave me my own collection

Jump when I say jump, girl can you take direction?

Mutombo with the bitches, you keep getting rejected.

A couple seconds later, Reek jumped in the passenger side. He reached for the 'L' and I looked at him like he had lost his rabbit ass mind. Yeah, I told him to come out and blow one with me but chiefing with him was the furthest thing from my mind.

63

Nah, see, what I wanted to do is pull the bitch from my waistband and burn him with it. A little voice in my mind was telling me to do just that. But another voice, someplace in the back of my mind, told me Reek was my brotha from a different motha and he wouldn't dare think about coming at me raw. That one place in the back of my mind resided a conscious I didn't have for anybody but him. Any other nigga would've been on the receiving end of my wrath a long time ago.

"I thought you wanted to burn, foo'," said Reek with his face scrunched up after he lowered the volume to my music.

I sat up, and turned the music back to the max. I eyed Reek from the corner of my eye and peeped him shaking his head. I closed my eyes and bobbed my head to the music as I continued to pull from the blunt. I was doing something I was good at. Scaring him. Intimidating him without uttering a word. Reek's the only nigga, besides Dawson, who knows me for real. And he know I'm on some ill shit right now. What he don't know is why. I'll inform him in a minute. Right na, though, I wanna finish my blunt. Alone. The fuck I look like burning one down with a nigga who might be snaking me?

I opened my eyes, and sat my seat back up. I took one more pull from the blunt before putting it out and sitting it in the ashtray. I turned the key and shifted the car in reverse. Reek went to touch my radio again, but I shot him a look that told him not to touch my shit. He

US AGAINST EVERYBODY: A DETROIT LOVE
TALE 2

waved me off and reclined his seat. He was acting casual
but I knew he was 'noid. Reek liked to pretend like he
wasn't fazed by me but he was. He just didn't want to
seem like a pussy by reacting to it.

After driving for twenty minutes, I was at my
destination and Reek was snoring. Stupid ass nigga fell
asleep not knowing what was about to come to him. Like
I said, he played that nonchalant role but the nigga was
really shook.

I parked between the trees and shifted the car in park
before shutting the engine off. I nudged him in the
shoulder and when he opened his eyes, he sat straight up
and looked out the windows.

"Nigga, wha—what the fuck we doing out here,"
asked Reek as looked out into the darkness of the woods.

I pulled my burner from my waistband and checked
it out, "To talk, my nigga. Get out."

I opened the door and hopped out. There was nothing
out here for about ten miles. We were in a secluded,
abandoned area surrounded by woods. It was so dark out
that you could barely make out what was in front of you.

65

I kept the headlights on to illuminate as much as possible. All I needed was enough light to hit my target if need be. Speaking of my target, he was still in the whip.

I banged on the roof of the car, "Get out nigga, the fuck you doing!?"

My heart was racing, and my palms were sweaty despite the fact that it was only about sixty degrees. My adrenaline was rushing. I got the same feeling every time before I murked me a nigga. I just hoped like fuck Reek wasn't going to make me off him.

He got out and said, "What the fuck we out here for, Vice? Stop playing me like I'm a nigga who don't know you dog." He was leaning on the roof of the car, looking over at me.

"You worried my nigga?" I asked as I slowly walked over to the side of his car.

"If you gone take me out, at least show me enough respect to tell me why," He said with his hands stuffed in his grey jogging pants.

I stood in his face and said, "Give me one reason why I shouldn't split yo wig open right now."

I pressed the chrome plated glock nine to the middle of his forehead. His body tensed up and I peeped the fear in his eyes. He could stand here on some unfazed shit all he wanted to. The eyes are windows to the soul. He was scared.

US AGAINST EVERYBODY: A DETROIT LOVE TALE 2

"Dog, I'm not about to stand here and…and tell you shit you already know! I've been here my nigga! Since day one! That paranoia got you vexed my nigga! I'm yo mothafuckin right hand man! Blood couldn't make this shit more triller. But it's aight! I feel you bro! In most cases it's always the nigga closest to you to betray you." Tears fell from his eyes as he bit on his bottom lip, "but that ain't the case right now, bro!" he cleared his throat and said, "Make it quick, yo."

He was just bluffing right? Trying to throw me off with them sucka ass crocodile tears. Nigga just bitchin up because I'm about to snatch the life up out of his disloyal ass. Look, I don't have any hard evidence against 'em but why do I need it? Shit, the slow up of all the bullshit that's been popping off after I murk him will be confirmation. But what if that don't happen? My nigga would be dead because of me. Damn, there goes that fuckin' conscious.

I yelled, "Shut the fuck up!"

I wasn't talking to Reek. I was talking to my conscious. I needed to get rid of that shit, pronto. I felt like I was off my game. The nigga standing before me

67

never gave me a reason to second guess his loyalty. We rocked hard as fuck together. Bro was there for whatever, whenever. We started this shit together. We started from the bottom together. Fuck!

I gritted my teeth and said to him, "Don't think because I'm a lil reluctant to pull the trigger now that that'd be the case if I really, really have to brodie!"

I walked away and got back in the car. Next time I pull the gun on him, I'm using it. I peeped Reek wipe his face with the sleeve of his long sleeve thermal top. He got in the car and I turned the key.

"This shit is way more than drug dealing for me, my nigga. This shit here was built on loyalty. The fuck I look like switching up? That fake shit ain't in my blood and if it's a nigga out here that should know that it's you, Vice. Don't insult me with that disloyal shit, yo. If it wasn't for you putting me on, I would've been in that shelter for I don't know how long. You looking out was some one hunnet, shit! Fuck I look like repaying you with disloyalty? I'm on the same mission as you. Ain't tryna compete or take yo spot." He paused and looked out the window, "You watch too many movies dawg."

"Shut yo crybaby ass up," I joked, trying to lighten the mood up.

"Dog, I saw my life flash before my eyes. You had murder all in yo pupils my nigga." He laughed, "Don't charge that shit to my gangsta though!"

US AGAINST EVERYBODY: A DETROIT LOVE TALE 2

And just like that, shit was back to normal. Like I didn't just have the banger to his dome.

*

I wanted to give her as much space as possible but somehow, I ended up at her spot. I couldn't even remember the drive there. My mind was all over the place. I needed lil' mama to ease my mind. I needed her to make the stress of this drug shit go away. Even if it would only be momentarily. I've never had a woman who made me feel the way Storm made me feel. The way she made a nigga feel all tingly inside was scary. I didn't like having a soft spot for her. But on the real, it's been that way since I met her. Most of the time, I can't believe the shit that's coming out of my mouth when I'm in her presence. I've been surprising myself left and right while fucking with her.

Yeah, I was in a relationship with Jos but that was different. She didn't make me feel like Storm makes me feel. Fuck, I don't even think I was in love with Jos. I've never uttered those three words to her. She told me but in return, I'd just nod with a smile. That's probably why she

69

hated Storm so much. She could peep how open brown skin had me and it had happened so fast.

I looked at the digital numbers on my dash, *4:00AM.* This was straight up booty call hours but I wasn't even here for all that. All I needed to do was lie next to her and my problems would fade away. That's all I needed the other night when she caught me in her bed. I just needed to be around lil' mama.

I called her and she answered.

"Vice?" she answered sounding groggy.

"Let me in."

She paused. Looking at the time, I assume.

"Vice it's four i—

"I know what time it is. But I need you right now, brown skin."

Last time I came through, she wasn't here so I climbed through an unlocked window. What? A nigga was desperate. My mood was fucked up that night. I wanted to go on a rampage all over the D. Even though she wasn't there, I knew she would be. And that calmed a nigga down. The smell of her on her pillow was good enough until I felt her lie beside me.

I stood on her porch, leaned up against the house, holding the phone to my ear. I heard moving in the background, then smiled. She was getting up. I took my

US AGAINST EVERYBODY: A DETROIT LOVE TALE 2

back off the house and stood at the door waiting for her to open up. A couple seconds later, she did, with the phone still pressed against her ear. I hung up and she held her phone in her hand looking up at me.

Although she was mad, I could peep the concern in her eyes. I opened the door and she held her arms open. Exactly what I needed right now. I leaned down a little and hugged her.

"Vice… I…can't breathe," said Storm with her arms wrapped around my neck.

I buried my face in her neck and inhaled. She always smelled good. Her morning breath even smelled good. I swear. A nigga could be bugging on some in love shit, but whatever yo. I eased up on my grip and told her she smelled good.

Storm kissed me on my cheek and I lifted her from her feet. As I carried her to her room, she lied her head on my chest and asked me if everything was okay. I told her shit was perfect right now. Things were always perfect when I was with her.

"I'm on my period," said Storm as I laid her on the bed.

"If I can walk through mud, I can fuck through blood," I said with a mischievous grin, as I took my jeans off.

She covered her mouth and said, "Oh my God. You nasty nigga!"

I cracked up laughing, "Keep calm brown skin. A nigga ain't even here to slide up in them guts. I just wanna feel ya lil' body up against mine. That's aight?"

She bashfully smiled, "Yes, baby."

I turned the light off and joined her in bed, "Baby huh? That mean you've made your mind up then huh?"

I pulled her body on top of mines and she kissed my neck, "Yes, I guess so."

"I knew you was fucking with a nigga regardless anyway," I playfully said as I rubbed the dip in her back.

She continued to kiss on my neck, "Cocky ass nigga."

"Uh huh! I just know you can't get enough of me, baby!" She laughed and softly bit my earlobe. I gripped her as cheeks and said, "Keep that shit up, and a nigga will be fucking through blood."

US AGAINST EVERYBODY: A DETROIT LOVE TALE 2

Storm told me I was nasty with a laugh before the room fell silent. Both of us in our thoughts. I concentrated to our heartbeats thumping in sync. That shit was kind of scary so I tried my damnedest to change the rhythm mine was beating in. Of course there was nothing I could do. Soon after, I drifted off to sleep.

*

A few hours later I woke up to Storm yelling. I grabbed my phone from the nightstand and checked the time, ignoring the missed calls and texts I had. *8:45AM.* Storm was getting ready for work. But whoever she was on the phone with had her pissed.

"I asked you to stop calling me! Nigga, ain't shit up! The only reason I called you was to get Ryan's number!"

I jumped out of bed and headed in the direction of her yelling. She was in the bathroom. I pushed the door open and stared at her reflection in the mirror before entering. She was naked with the exception of a pair of panties. On her face she wore a frown as she tried to fill her eyebrows in. I pushed the door completely open, startling her.

73

She dropped her eyeliner in the sink and I took the phone from her ear.

"I was just trying to upgrade yo basic ass, bitch," said the disrespectful nigga on the other end of the phone.

"Who this," I asked with a smile on my face.

Storm shook her head and hunched her shoulders as she continued to paint her face with makeup she didn't need.

"B! Who the fuck is this?"

I hung up. He'll find out soon enough. I'm sick of that weak ass nigga. I should've bodied his ass a long time ago. I stood behind Storm and whispered in her ear, "Get your number changed, aight? I don't need weak niggas hitting your line. Feel me?"

She pressed her ass on my crotch and said, "Mmhmm, I feel you."

I knew what she meant but now wasn't the time for that play-play shit. I needed her to be serious.

I grabbed her waist and told her, "I'm serious, Storm. Get a new number."

She looked at me with a frown, "Okay, meanie."

"I'm not being mean, baby. I just telling you. Nigga won't be breathing for much longer, but while he is, I don't want him calling you aight?"

US AGAINST EVERYBODY: A DETROIT LOVE TALE 2

"Alright, Vice."

I smacked her on the ass and told her to have a great day at work before heading back to the room. She told me she loved me and for some reason I hesitated to say it back. I love lil' mama for sure, but saying those words made me feel eerie.

*

After getting four more hours a sleep, I woke up to my ringing phone. I grabbed the phone and shook my head at the pretty light skin face looking back at me. I made a mental note to delete the pics I had of Joslyn from my phone.

I sat up and rubbed sleep from my eyes before answering.

"Yo?"

"Good morning, bighead," said Joslyn in a cheery voice.

"What do you want?"

75

She sucked her teeth, "I just wanted to let you know that I'm all settled in my crib. I wanted you to come by. Not on no fuck shit. Just to show you my spot."

"Send me a picture, Jos. Bye."

"Wait, wait, wait!" I shook my head and she continued, "Please just come by."

"I'll let you know."

I heard the smile on her face as she talked, "Okay. Hit me up later? I'ma text you the address."

"Aight, Jos," was all I said before hanging up on her.

A few seconds later my notifications went off. She wasted no time sending the address. I wasn't going to check her spot out though. She was having a hard time understanding that I wasn't fucking with her ass like that no more.

After replying to a few text messages and returning calls, I got up and headed to the bathroom for a shower. I had some business to take care of. First on my list was to hit up a few of my blocks on six mile. Word was, that some off brand nigga kept coming through trying to set up shop. My soldiers over there weren't letting that shit fly though. Still, I wanted to post up for a lil bit to see if the nigga would pop up. I knew he would because Marko – a worker over there – said he came through daily. I prayed he didn't choose not to today. I needed to burn a nigga. I was itching to get a niggas blood on me.

US AGAINST EVERYBODY: A DETROIT LOVE TALE 2

*

An hour later I was riding down Caldwell, bumping Flex by Rich Homie Quan. The block was jumping. Kids were out playing despite the fact that it was school hours on a Monday afternoon. Their thot ass momma's didn't care. Not one bit. They sat on the porch loud and ratchet, smoking on blunts and drinking cheap ass liquor from the bottle. As I drove past they threw their hands up and yelled wassup. I just nodded at them. What a fucking disgrace.

I parked a few houses down from the trap and shut my engine off. I was solo dolo. Although Reek and I were cool, the nigga was still pretty heated. I couldn't blame 'em though. I was always pulling the banger out on him. I could've been making a mistake by not pulling the trigger. But like I said, next time I pull it on him I'm offing him. If I get a next time. If he don't get me before I him. A nigga couldn't help but be paranoid. Can you blame me? I'm out here playing a dirty game.

I hopped out of the car and headed down the block to the spot. Like I said, the block was jumping. Fetty Wap blasted from a house with a porch full of people who said wassup to me. I returned the greeting and shook my head at the thot bitch twerking in the face of a young nigga who looked to be about ten years old. Obviously no one found anything wrong with that because they all were laughing, cheering the bitch on.

I jogged up the stairs to the spot. Before I could open the door to walk in, someone inside opened it for me.

I slapped hands with Marko, "What it is, young boi!?"

Marko's one of the coolest niggas I have on payroll. He keeps shit over here moving swiftly. I never have any issues with this house. It might not accumulate as much cheese as the crib on Riopelle but trust, a nigga eating!

We sat on the beaten up faux leather couch and he said, "Getting to the money, boss, you know how it be."

A couple young niggas in back of the house yelled wassup and I spoke back.

"Dude been through the block yet?"

Marko scratched his nappy ass fro, "Hell nah. He'll be through though. Mark my words bro." he lifted his pull over sweater up exposing a gun, "I got something for his ass this time though."

"Hold off on that. I'm glad you ain't already pulled his cap back. I want to get at boi myself."

US AGAINST EVERYBODY: A DETROIT LOVE TALE 2

Marko nodded, went in his pocket and retrieved a sponge and ran it over his fro, putting more naps in it. I chuckled. I couldn't understand why niggas liked that stupid looking shit. All the hood niggas were wearing the same style. Me, I couldn't get with that shit. I didn't want to look like everybody else.

I pulled my phone from my pocket and texted Storm:

ME (2:12PM): hope you're having a bomb ass day, lil mama.

STORM (2:13PM): LOL. Yea, bae I'm having a bomb ass day.

ME (2:13PM): Chill with that soft ass bae shit. Mack might be yo father but I'm daddy.

I laughed out loud and Marko gave me a weird look. I cleared my throat and put my phone back in my pocket. Brown skin had me out here on some soft shit. As weird as shit made me feel, I couldn't help but wear a stupid ass grin on my face.

"Damn, boss, she gotta sister," asked Marko with a smirk on his face.

That wiped the grin right off my face. I couldn't let these niggas know a chick had me open like this. That shit served as a weakness. I didn't want anybody knowing I had a soft spot period. A nigga with larceny in his heart would pounce on the opportunity to use her against me quick as hell.

"What nigga," I asked with a stone cold mug on my face.

The look I gave caused him to shift in his seat. He told me never mind and got up from the couch. Fuck 'em, fuck his feelings. He a cool ass nigga but there are lines that I won't tolerate being crossed. We can bull shit around all day. But don't inquire about my girl in any way period.

Damn, dog, I can't fuck with Storm while I'm out handling business. These niggas don't need to see anything but the thug in me. It's kind of hard not to hit her up when I'm away from her. Lil' mama is constantly on my mental. I'm going to have to learn how to push her lil' sexy ass in the back of my mind. I never had this problem fucking with Jos. I knew how to separate the two. When I was handling business Joslyn didn't even exist. This…this is different.

"Nigga pulling up now, boss," said Marko standing at the front door with his hand on his burner.

I walked up on him and said, "Chill on that gunplay nigga. I got this shit."

US AGAINST EVERYBODY: A DETROIT LOVE TALE 2

"I'm saying though, let me put the work in! You kick back. Let me body this nigga," he bit on his bottom lip as he intensely glared out of the window.

"Just fall back, cuz," I told him with a screwed look on my face.

Marko was hungry to catch a body. I didn't mind adding another name to the list of niggas I sent off, neither but I wasn't itching like this fool here. He's a young hot headed cat. His eagerness to kill is flattering as fuck but I don't need a nigga putting in work for me. I get my hands dirty. I add bodies to the burner.

I pushed Marko to the side just as ol' boy opened his car door. I ran down the steps, and before he could step out I was standing at his door.

As soon as he looked up at me he shifted the car in drive and sped off. He knew what the fuck was up. He knew he'd already had a death wish on him. Fuck nigga Storm use to talk to, same nigga she was cussing out earlier. Pussy ass boi!

I looked up at the house at Marko, and three other niggas, standing on the porch.

"Fuck was that about?" asked Marko, staring at the car speed away.

"Nigga's a bitch," I walked towards my car, "If he come back through, which I doubt he will, keep him here and hit me up."

Marko nodded and told me to stay up. I told him to keep his eyes and ears on the streets.

*

I switched the track to Digital Dash by Future and Drake. I drove the streets of Detroit in my Bvlgari shades, music blasting, and windows down. I was on a mission. I had to find out where that nigga rested. I don't even know shit about the nigga, but what I did know is that he frequently went to The Crazy Horse. So that's where I'm headed. I wanted to hit Storm up and see what she knew but I didn't want her in this shit. I wanted to keep this life away from her as much as possible. I already almost lost Shorty because of that shootout. A shootout I don't know shit about. A lot of mothafuckas wanted me dead. And to be honest, I'm pretty much to blame.

I walked around the D without a care in the world. I intimidated and bitched a lot of niggas. Most of the time in front of their bitches or their fam. Tank – Lando's bro – and his camp could be behind all of these shootouts. I rode up on them niggas knowing they knew I killed ol'

US AGAINST EVERYBODY: A DETROIT LOVE TALE 2

boy. I bitched them in a time of sorrow. I couldn't give a fuck less about their feelings, though. So I could easily place the shootout on Tank. I could place the blame on B too. I bitched him on several occasions. Let's not get on the shit I did before I met you. I'm a young wild, ignorant nigga.

As I drove around the city, I thought about what Reek said a couple months ago. He said I needed to chill on that wild shit. I needed to, but fuck… we all bleed the same. When I did crazy shit I felt invincible. And if a nigga catch me slipping then it is what it is. I stay on my P's and Q's though so if a nigga ever catch me slippin, bet bread I won't fall. I'm just living life ya know? I can't walk around here worried about dying. Dying is inevitable. We all gotta die someway. It'd be some gangsta ass shit to go out like Scarface though.

I laughed to myself and pulled into The Crazy Horse's parking lot. I shut the engine off and headed inside.

Get a plastic bag

Gone ahead and pick up all the cash

Gone ahead and pick up all the cash

You danced all night, girl, you deserve it

Get a plastic bag

Gone ahead and pick up all the cash

Gone ahead and pick up all the cash

You danced all night, girl, you deserve it.

I walked into the club without paying. Niggas showed love like that, although I didn't need it. From the speakers played Plastic Bag off my favorite mixtape, What a Time to Be Alive. The club was banging. Bitches flocked to me but I ignored them. I was looking for Ginger. If there was anybody I could get information from it was her nosey ass.

Ginger is a waitress but niggas fuck with her heavy. She prance around the club acting as if all she's doing is taking orders, but in reality her ass is ear hustling too. I know how these waitresses get down so I never talked business while I was out.

I stood at the bar and looked to my right. Genie was sitting there in her street clothes, sipping from a glass of liquor. Her eyes were glossed over. I could tell off rip, that she was high off her eyes. She licked her plum colored lips and turned her head my way.

"Wassup my baby," asked Genie with a smile.

US AGAINST EVERYBODY: A DETROIT LOVE TALE 2

I nodded, "What's good?"

"That new shit you got," she stood up from her stool and stood beside me, "Keep that shit, bro."

"You know how I get down, Genie. Stop talking."

"Anyway," she waved me off, "You heard anything from Jai?"

She didn't know I fucked with Jai's best friend, but she knew I knew Jai.

"Nah, what happened up here that night though?"

To my knowledge, Genie is the only broad up here that Jai fucks with heavy. If there's anybody that knows what happened it's her loose ass.

Genie shook her head, "Bitch was doing too fucking much! Stupid ass ho." She laughed, "Nah," she looked over her shoulder then whispered, "That's what I got her thinking." She put her finger to her lip and said, "Shhh. I had to get that pretty red bitch up out of here. She was stealing my clientele. Ho was starting to feel herself to much. Feel me bro? I had to eliminate the competition.

Plus the bitch thought she was too good to get her pussy licked on by me."

I chuckled and shook my head, "You know Genie," I bit my bottom lip and tapped her forehead with my finger, "You talk too fucking much."

She jerked her head away and fixed her Chinese bang, "What?"

I laughed, "Stay up out here, Gen. You know how dangerous it can be out here for bitches like you." I winked and walked away to look for Ginger.

A nigga ain't saying shit, but aye, ain't no telling what the fuck the future holds for her. I fucks with Storm, and Storm fucks with Jai. Shorty is family.

Shortly after, I found Ginger in the back of the club taking orders. I told her to come holla at me in the whip. It didn't take her long to come out. And when she did, she gave me an ear full. She told me exactly what I needed to hear. Like how B slanged dope in HP. For Oozy.

[FIVE]

Storm

"**A**lright, girl, I'll holla at you later," I told Carla as we got into our cars.

The work day was over and I was happy as hell. I couldn't wait to get out of there. Unfortunately, I wasn't going straight home. But, hell, anything is better than being at work. My hair is looking 'bout raggedy as hell. I took my sew-in out last night. My ass was at work rocking a beanie. Carla's friend sells Mink Brazilian hair, and she brought it to work with her. I didn't mind spending five hundred dollars on hair. Especially since it was five hundred of Vice's dollars.

I hopped on the freeway, heading to the hood. I had a hard time keeping my eyes open. Vice coming over so late last night messed my sleeping up. I didn't mind though. There was nothing more satisfying than waking up to him. Maybe I will take him up on that offer of moving in together.

Fifteen minutes later, I was parking in front of the hair salon. I texted my stylist, Mia, to let her know I was here. She told me she stepped out and that her home girl would start on my head. I told her ass she'd better hurry up because I wasn't cool with just anybody in my hair.

I grabbed my purse and hair from the passenger seat and then headed inside. As usual, it was crowded but that didn't have shit to do with me – I have an appointment.

I sat in Mia's chair, scrolling down my Instagram timeline as I waited. I planned on going to see Jai before visiting hours were over. Since I braided my hair up already, this would take no time if Mia hurried her ass up.

"Hey, you have the four o'clock appointment with Mia," she extended her hand, "I'm...."

Before she could get her name out, we locked eyes and I knew exactly who she was. Joslyn. Vice's ex.

I stood up and laughed, "Aw hell naw! Mia gotta bring her ass on. You ain't touching my fucking hair. The fuck!"

Joslyn stepped back and rolled her eyes, "Yeah, ok and, bitch!? Like I actually want to. While you popping off at the mouth, you can get the fuck out!"

US AGAINST EVERYBODY: A DETROIT LOVE TALE 2

By then we had the attention of the entire shop. The three girls that walked up and stood behind Joslyn grabbed my attention. The bitch had a squad with her. While I'm standing here solo, dolo out numbered.

I wasn't intimidated at all!

"Ho please! You don't own this shop! Fuck out of here with yo mad ass," I giggled and turned my attention to my phone, getting ready to call Mia.

"Shit sweet BF," asked one of the bitches with Joslyn.

Joslyn smirked and nodded her head before saying, "Yeah, this ugly bitch just mad because her nigga can't leave me alone."

"Aight, look...I'm not gone be too many of your bitches," I calmly said after putting my phone in my purse.

I don't know what gave her courage. Bitch must've drunk some crunk juice or some shit. She had to be off something to grow balls big enough to step into my personal space. She gazed down at my smiling face as I sat my bag on the floor.

"What you gon' do? Besides get yo ass beat, bi—

Before she could get the 'tch' out, I hit her square in the mouth. I didn't give her a chance to recover before I was pounding on her. She might've been thicker and taller than me, but I was wailing on her ass. I grabbed a fist full of her hair, and yanked her down to my level. Just as I began to pound on her face, her three friends jumped in and I fell to the floor pulling Joslyn right down with me.

Instead of pulling the bitches off of me, the people in the shop stood by recording everything. Although they were beating my ass, I kept my grip on Joslyn. I was going to do damage to at least one of them. As her friends beat on the back of my head and body, I kept landing punches on Joslyn. I dug my nails into her face with one hand, and punched her with the other. Her friends began to stomp on me and I didn't have any choice but to release her. Joslyn crawled from beneath me and joined in on the jumping.

"What the hell is going on," I heard Mia yelling.

I kicked and punched while I laid on the floor as they dragged and punched me. Just as one of them was bringing their Jordan down on my face, she was pulled away by Mia and some big burly man. The man threw the remaining three off of me and I managed to stand.

US AGAINST EVERYBODY: A DETROIT LOVE TALE 2

"Storm, I'm so so—

I cut Mia off and yelled, "Weak ass bitches jump! I'ma catch each and every last one of you ho's out in these streets. BET THAT BITCH." I was trying to get at them, but whoever the man with Mia was held me back.

"Let me go, nigga!"

He looked down at me and said, "Relax. You need to calm down. Your head is busted."

I touched my forehead and went charging at them again. But by then, Mia was making them leave as she cursed everyone out. She kept apologizing to me but it wasn't her fault. I was so fucking heated. I couldn't believe that, once again, I was in some shit because of Vice.

I yanked away from the guy and walked out of the shop despite Mia calling after me. She wanted to do my hair. She said she'd do it for free because of what happened but I ignored her. I wanted to be as far away from that shop as possible. I was heated. Very fucking heated.

91

As I sat behind the wheel of my car, I cried. Not because I was sad but because I couldn't believe I just got jumped. I haven't been in anything like this since high school. All I seen was red. I wanted each and every last one of those bitches dead. As much as I'd like to believe that I was overreacting, I couldn't deny that the feeling of wanting them dead wasn't real. It was real alright. My shaking hands, and bouncing leg was confirmation.

I yanked my phone from my purse and called Vice.

"Wassup, lil' baby?"

I rolled my eyes and yelled, "Where that bitch live at?" I started the car and forcefully drove out of the parking lot.

"Whoa, whoa. Slow down brown skin, what's going on?"

"Yo bitch and her friends just fucking jumped me!"

He paused and a certain calmness, that irritated me, came over his voice, "Storm, I don't have any bitches. Where are you?"

"Riding! Where she live? You can chill on that you don't have any bitches shit too! The bitch said you couldn't leave her alone! I'm in the shop getting dragged and jumped because of you!" I beat on the steering wheel, "Because of you! Once again! Damn I wish I didn't love you!"

US AGAINST EVERYBODY: A DETROIT LOVE TALE 2

"Don't say that. Don't speak shit you really don't mean while you're upset. Calm the fuck down," he said in that same calm fucking voice like he really didn't give a shit about what just happened to me.

I laughed and made a sharp right onto seven mile, "You don't even care! Your bi—

He yelled, "Ay, on some real shit, stop calling that broad my bitch! Calm yo hot ass down, yo! You acting crazy won't do shit but cause you to get into a fucking accident. Calm. Down! Fuck you mean I don't care?! What? Because I'm not wilding out like you. Stop making me yell at you, brown skin," he paused, "You know I don't like this shit."

I sighed and pulled over on side of the road, "Vice, they beat me up bad." I tried to swallow the lump in my throat, "Four bitches on me. FOUR! Mad because I was beating the whole fuck out yo bi—I mean Joslyn."

I heard him grit his teeth, "Go home."

"What?"

"Go home. I'll be there in two hours."

93

"What?" Silence. "Hello?"

I looked at my phone and he had hung up.

*

As I was standing in my full length mirror looking at all of the bruises on my body, he walked in. Like clockwork, he was there in two hours. Vice stood behind me, staring into my eyes as his hands touched the bruises on my body. His eyes were full of raging sadness. He bit on his bottom lip and closed his eyes, as he buried his face in my neck inhaling. He always smelled me. And it always made me smile. As pissed as I was, he put a smile on my face.

Vice turned me to face him and touched the small gash on my forehead. Again, he closed his eyes. This time he exhaled deeply before pulling me into his arms.

"Are you ready," he asked, speaking into my neck.

I pulled away and asked him, "For what?"

"To see the side of me I've been trying to hide from you?"

"Huh?"

"Get dressed," said Vice before leaving the room.

US AGAINST EVERYBODY: A DETROIT LOVE
TALE 2

I stood there, baffled. I shook my head and went to
my dresser to throw on a pair of yoga pants and a tank.
On my feet were a pair of Nike flip flops. I looked in the
mirror once more and tears welled up into my eyes.

"Stop that crying," said Vice startling me. I didn't
even know he was standing in the doorway. "And change
your shoes."

"Where are we going," I asked as I kicked my flip
flops off and put some socks on.

"For a ride. Come on, lil' mama."

After putting on a pair of Jordan's we left.

The entire ride, I kept asking him where we were
headed. He just ignored me and talked about other things.
I was starting to get irritated. He asked me how Jai was
and everything. A part of me wanted to believe he
genuinely cared. But the other part of me knew he was
only asking to avoid answering my question. Maybe he
did care about Jai. I don't know. All I gave a fuck about
at the moment was where we were going.

We were downtown, parking in front of a condo. I looked up at the house and asked him where we were. Vice smiled and unbuckled my seatbelt before doing his. He told me to just wait and see. He got out of the car and then walked over and opened mine. I've learned to just sit there and wait. In the past, if I got out without him opening the door for me, he made me get back in so that he could. I thought it was corny. He thought it was a way to allow him to take care of me as I should be taken care of.

He grabbed my hand and we walked up to the house. Before he twisted the doorknob he turned to me and said, "I asked you earlier if you were ready." He paused and looked me square in the eyes, "Are you?"

I swallowed hard before asking, "What do you mean?"

"It's a simple question, baby. Are you ready to meet the side of me I've been trying to keep away from you?"

I hesitated, "Vice. What the fuck—

He cut me off, "Just answer the question Storm. Because if not, we can turn back around and go back to the crib. I won't even show you what's on the other side of the door."

But I wanted to know. The whole ride here, I inquired about where we were going. Ain't no way in hell I'm about to turn around now. I had not a clue of what

US AGAINST EVERYBODY: A DETROIT LOVE TALE 2

was behind the door. Shit, it could've been a dead body. Hell, it could've been my daddy's dead body. Aw shit. What the fuck? Nah, that's pushing it. I'm being noid. The only way for me to really find out is to suck it up and tell him I'm ready. I don't even know what the hell he actually means.

"Yeah, I'm ready."

He smiled and said, "Aight, bet."

Vice opened the door and when I laid my eyes on what was inside, I gasped.

Joslyn was ass naked, gagged, and tied to a chair. She looked over at us with tears falling from her eyes, which were full of fear. Think I gave a fuck? Nope. Not one bit. There wasn't an ounce of sympathy within me. I actually smiled. She deserved whatever was coming to her.

I turned to Vice and asked, "What is this?"

He pulled a gun from his waistband and I watched him in awe.

"It's whatever you want it to be, brown skin." He looked down at his Rolex, "But we gotta make whatever that is, fast."

I nodded and walked over to Joslyn who, with her eyes, pleaded with me. Oh? She wants mercy? Did her and her friends give me mercy as they stomped and beat on me? If the weak bitch would've taken her ass whooping like a real woman she wouldn't be in this predicament. If her friends would've minded their own fucking business she wouldn't be tied to a chair wondering if today was her last day on earth.

I snatched the tape from her mouth, watching as her lipstick came off with it. The first thing that left her mouth was please don't kill me.

I kneeled down in front of her and asked, "Why shouldn't I?"

This wasn't me. I'm not use to this type of shit but I won't lie and say it doesn't feel good. Joslyn's life was in my hands. All I had to do is turn to my man and tell him to blow her brains out. I turned to him and smiled. He stood there with the burner to his side, watching us. His eyes were fixated on Joslyn though. I saw something there. He felt betrayed by her. Although they had history, he wouldn't hesitate to end her. I wondered how true that was. He stood there with the burner but I wasn't one hundred percent sure he'd murk her if that's what I wanted. He knew her before me. They had history.

US AGAINST EVERYBODY: A DETROIT LOVE TALE 2

"Baby," I called for him.

He walked over to us and wrapped his arms around me, "What it is, lil mama?"

I looked over my shoulder into his hazels, "Should we kill her?"

Vice shrugged his shoulders and asked, "Jos, should we kill you my baby?" Vice let go of me and lightly pushed me aside so that he was standing directly in front of her, "What you think, bitch? I mean hell, a nigga looked out for you on some one hundred shit on different occasions. You know brown skin is my lady. You know firsthand how I feel about mothafuckas who disrespect me. You had to know I was gone act a fucking nut once I found out you and yo rat ass friends put hands on her." He looked over his shoulder at me, "Look at her Jos! LOOK AT WHAT THE FUCK YOU BUM BITCHES DID!" He grabbed her face and made her look at me.

Joslyn sobbed louder, "S-storm I'm so sorry. So sorry! Please don't hurt me Vice."

No matter how pissed I might be, this ain't me. I tapped Vice on the shoulder and asked if we could talk for a minute. I wanted Joslyn dead but I didn't want to be responsible. I hated her and her friends for what she did to me. I wanted to test Vice. Just to see if he'd really kill for me. I got my answer. He would. I could tell he no longer cared about the history him and Joslyn shared by the way he spoke to her. Nothing but hate dripped from his tongue as he spoke to her. Vice spoke in a tone I've never heard him speak. He was disgusted. He felt betrayed. And Vice was a man who didn't tolerate betrayal.

"What's wrong baby? You wanna off her? You sure you ready? You know I can handle that shit though," he handed me the gun and I shook my head.

"I don't want to kill her, Vice."

He frowned, "Fuck you mean!? She...her and her friends...look at you man! Look at your beautiful face!" he was furious. So furious that his body was trembling, and his eye twitching.

I placed my hands on the sides of his face, "Shhh. It's okay. I don't want you to kill her but I do want you to scare the shit out of her."

"Storm...this...I don't let shit like this slide."

"I know. But this is my beef not y—

"Your beef is my beef. What you speakin bout, girl? Bitch did this to you out of jealousy!" he grabbed my

US AGAINST EVERYBODY: A DETROIT LOVE TALE 2

hands and said, "No one is allowed to put their hands on you. You understand me? No one!"

I've never seen Vice so mad. He was scaring me a little. I just wanted him to calm down. I needed him to listen to me. But it was like he didn't care about what I was saying. It seem like there was no changing his mind. Vice's mind was made up regardless of what I wanted.

"You asked me what I wanted, Vice. Remember?"

"Respect is what you want, Storm. Respect. And when this bitch come up missing mothafuckas will know." He turned in Joslyn's direction, "They will know you're not to be fucked with. No one is exempt."

I grabbed him, "You ain't wasting bullets on that bitch, aight!?!"

His head jerked in my direction and he smiled, "You boss huh? Damn you look good. Being all bossy and shit." He grabbed my waist and said, "Got a nigga dick hard as fuck, brown skin."

"Stop playing Vice. I'm serious."

He bit his bottom lip and said, "Aight, well, peep. Let me have a lil' fun with this disloyal bitch."

"Wait."

I walked away from him and back to Joslyn. I kneeled down and untied her from the chair. I wanted this bitch to square up with me and take this ass beating.

I stood up and said, "Come on bitch, let's go."

"What," she asked through her sobs.

I put my hands up, "Come get this work, ho! Stand up."

Vice looked at me like I was crazy, "Storm, fuck is you doing baby?"

Instead of replying to him, I punched Joslyn in her eye. She covered it and yelled out in pain. I thought I'd stop there but something clicked in my mind and I went crazy on her. I stood over her, beating all over her body. I kicked the chair and she fell to the floor. She put her hands up to shield her face and that reminded me of how I was a few hours ago. I couldn't stop the heavy flow of tears that fell from my eyes as I stomped on her.

After a few seconds, Vice scooped me up and said that was enough. I walked away and stood against the wall, breathing heavily. He stared at me briefly before pulling the gun from his waistband again and walking

US AGAINST EVERYBODY: A DETROIT LOVE TALE 2

away. I didn't have the strength or care enough to stop him that time.

He stood over Joslyn's naked body, gawking down at her as she cried. He asked her why she'd made the stupid ass decision to jump his girl.

"She...she hit me and they...they jumped in. It wasn't my fault V-v-vice. Please don't kill me! I love yo—

He cut her off, "Shut the fuck up, Joslyn!" Vice roughly pulled Joslyn's legs open and I took my back off the wall. He looked over his shoulder at me and said, "I can't murk this bitch, brown skin?"

I just shrugged my shoulders. I didn't know what the fuck he was about to do to her. He nodded and in one swift motion, entered the gun into her pussy. I gasped and ran over to him. He looked at me and said, "Shhh."

I shivered in fear. Joslyn was hysterical. Crying, and confessing her love for him. That shit rubbed me wrong. So wrong that I couldn't stop my foot from coming in contact with her face. What the hell was happening to me? When I kicked her, I told her to shut the fuck up.

I've never been this brutal in my life. I've whooped my share of ass but this was different.

Vice looked her in the eyes as he spoke, "Joslyn. Look at me, baby girl."

Through eyes clouded with tears, she did as she was told.

He 'fucked' her with the gun with his finger on the trigger, as he spoke, "You know how I feel about Storm, ain't that right?" Joslyn nodded and he continued, "You…you and your bum ass friends should've never put y'all filthy hands on her. Look at her!" Joslyn didn't turn my way and he yelled for her to look at me again. She did and he continued to taunt her, "She's beautiful! She's like a rare diamond or some shit. You think you special enough to put hands on her? Fuck no! You shouldn't even be looking her way but I had to make a point. Look at me Joslyn." She looked at him again and he licked his lips and continued, "My finger on this trigger feels good as fuck man. I just…I'm itching to pull it."

I touched him on the shoulder and said, "Don't."

Vice looked up at me and said, "But my baby, my sexy lil brown skin, she said I can't kill you." He shoved the gun further inside her and moved closer to her face, "But peep this shit though Jos. If I have any more issues out of you or yo thot ass friends, what Storm says won't matter. I wish it didn't matter now but I love her so I'm

US AGAINST EVERYBODY: A DETROIT LOVE TALE 2

willing to compromise." He smiled and pulled the gun from her vagina before standing.

Joslyn curled up into fetal position and continued to sob uncontrollably.

"Tell wifey you're sorry, bitch," said Vice standing behind me with his hands on my waist.

"I apologi—

"I said, tell her you're sorry!"

She flinched and told me she was sorry.

Vice nodded and we walked out of the house.

Instead of being afraid, I felt excitement. I loved every side of him. Instead of shying away from it; I embraced the craziness.

When we got in the car he grabbed my chin and turned me his way.

"Understand that I'll cause havoc out to this bitch over you," he kissed me on the forehead, "I love you brown skin, on my momma."

"I know. And I love you too, Vice."

US AGAINST EVERYBODY: A DETROIT LOVE
TALE 2

[SIX]
Jai

Three weeks had passed and I was fully recovered. I couldn't go back to dancing yet but in about a week or so I planned on doing just that, despite what everyone thought was best. Of course, Ryan knew I lied to him about quitting. Storm had to tell him everything. He was pissed at me. Even more pissed that I wanted to go back. I wasn't lying to his ass anymore. I told him the real.

Now he's at my place sitting across from me frowning. I tried my best to ignore him as I went down my Twitter feed. He was staring so fucking hard at me though. I looked up at him and realized that it wasn't me he was staring at. It was the tattoo on my wrist he was gawking at. The tat that clearly read 'gold digger'. The one I was supposed to cover up at all times when he was

107

around. I forgot though. I had so much shit on my mind. Like my coke for instance.

I took my hand from the table and sat it in my lap.

Ryan stood up and came on my side of the table. He grabbed my arm and stared at the tattoo.

"What is this about," he calmly asked.

I yanked my arm away, "What the fuck you mean what's it about? It's just a silly tattoo I got when I was younger."

He laughed, "You expect me to believe that you got that tat just for the fuck of it?" he huffed, "Come on now, Jai. I might be a sucker for a pretty face, bomb head, and good ass pussy but I'm not dumb." He nodded, "You've been playing me all along."

"Ain't nobody been playing yo—

"Well explain to me why this is my first time seeing the shit and we've been kicking it for months now, Jai!? You've been hiding it from me." He grabbed his Al Wissam leather off the chair and put it on. "You've been fucking with me with ill intentions. Bitch, you've been using me."

When the word bitch rolled off his tongue, my stomach dropped. Ryan has never talked to me like that. He's always been so sweet and caring. I couldn't believe I was actually hurt. I've never been hurt. I've never

US AGAINST EVERYBODY: A DETROIT LOVE TALE 2

allowed a man to get anywhere near my heart. All I cared about was benji's lacing my pockets. The fact that I was hurt told me that it was more than just money with Ryan.

I stood up, "What? Nigga you bugging! Use you for what? I have my own fucking money!"

He waved me off and walked away. I was on his heels. He was trying to leave and I couldn't have that. Usually, I wouldn't even be on this tip. I wouldn't give a damn about a nigga throwing a hissy fit and leaving. I'd let him do just that. But something was pulling me towards Ryan. I couldn't let that meal ticket walk away. That's what my mind was telling me but my heart was saying something different. My heart was telling me that, he's who I needed. Despite being ugly. He's who I wanted and not because of the money.

I stood in front of the door, blocking him in.

"Come on now, Jai, get out of my way. Let me go, shawty," said Ryan with a frown on his face.

"No."

That's all I could say. I didn't have anything catchy or alluring to say to persuade him. I just needed him to stay.

He lightly pushed me aside but I didn't move.

"Yo lil' ass already know I could easily get you out of my way. I don't want to be rough with you, Jai. Don't make me hurt you, alright? You just got out of the hospital. Just let a nigga go," He said with pain written all over his face.

"But, I don't want you to leave."

"Why not? So you can keep using me like my ex bitch did?" he shook his head and tried to push me away again.

"Stop! No. I just...I want you here Ryan."

"Tell me why, Jai. Give me a legit reason other than money as to why you want to fuck with me."

I stood there silent for a few seconds. I knew the answer to his question but I couldn't bring myself to say it. I wanted him for who he is. He was so delicate with me. He treated me so good. Unlike the thug niggas I was used to, he genuinely cared about me. He looked passed my flaws and stood by my side. Ryan knew I dapped in coke. Instead of running away, he wanted to help. He knew I shook my ass for cash. But he wanted to help me stop.

US AGAINST EVERYBODY: A DETROIT LOVE TALE 2

"Exactly." He lifted me from my feet and moved me from the door.

Before I could get there to block it again, he was walking out.

Like a crazy woman, I ran after him. I was outside in my bra and panties, and a bonnet. Ryan stopped walking down the steps, looked over his shoulder at me and shook his head. He told me to go back inside but I stood there. I didn't care. He waved me off again and continued to leave.

I yelled, "So you're going to leave me nigga?! Really!?"

"Yes, that's exactly what I'm going to do. You ain't about to keep using me."

What is this? I touched my face and it was wet. Wet from tears. What the fuck? I don't cry over men. Especially those who are willingly leaving me. I don't do this. What is this? Why am I running after him? I was running down the stairs and up to his car.

I shivered as I stood there banging on his window. He looked up at me and rolled the window down, "Jai go inside, you're going to be sick."

I wiped my face and said, "Ryan, I want you for you. I don't care about the money."

He laughed, "Typical. When you see I'm serious you say what you think I want to hear. Gone on somewhere, shawty." He shifted his car in drive, "Take care of yourself, okay?"

I stepped back and wrapped my arms around my body as I watched him drive away.

*

Three hours had passed and I was still in my feelings. I needed some coke but Vice wouldn't let anybody sell to me. So I was getting liquored up waiting on my best bitch to get here. What I really wanted to do is make my way to HP. Vice didn't have any clout over there so those niggas would serve me with no problem. I didn't know them neither which was why I was so skeptical.

I sat on the couch, taking shots of 1800 back-to-back. I needed to get the fuck up out of this house. I was thinking too much. I was tripping. I've called Ryan at least twelve times and was sent to voicemail each time. He was really done with a bitch and that drove me crazy.

US AGAINST EVERYBODY: A DETROIT LOVE TALE 2

I couldn't understand why I was falling for him. I've fucked with better looking niggas with racks on racks. What's so damn special about his ugly ass? He ain't the first ugly nigga I've messed with neither. He just might be the ugliest though. I know I sound shallow. Duh! I am shallow.

Bang! Bang!

"Let us in, bitch!"

Us? I know she ain't got Carla with her. Ugh, it was like we couldn't have sister time anymore. Carla was everywhere. She's cool as hell but I didn't like Storm having another friend. I wouldn't dare call her Storm's best friend. I was her one and only. Yeah, I'm territorial. All best friends are.

I got up and staggered to the door. I opened it and hugged my bitch. We rocked left and right like we haven't seen each other in weeks. When in all actuality, I just saw her three days ago.

As I hugged Storm, I looked Carla up and down and said, "Wassup, trick?"

Carla flipped me the bird and walked inside. I laughed. We did each other like that all the time. She knew I didn't want anybody else friends with Storm and she didn't give a fuck. Carla payed my shade throwing no mind. Her big head ass threw it right back.

We walked in the house and I closed the door behind us.

"You started without us, bitch!? Damn!" yelled Storm holding the damn near empty bottle of 1800 up.

"Y'all ho's were taking way too long," I said as I sat on the couch with them.

"We could've been coming from right down the street and that bottle would still be damn near empty like it is now. You know this broad drink like a fish Storm," said Carla while laughing.

I gave her the side eye, "Yeah okay, ho."

We laughed and joked around until it was time for Empire to come on. We sat laughing around eating strawberries and taking shots. After we finished off the bottle of 18, we cracked open the bottle of Effen. Usually, Storm wouldn't get so bent knowing she was driving. She and Carla were spending the night. Once I called and told her how fucked up Ryan had me she called an 'emergency sleepover'. What I didn't know was that Carla would be a part of it.

US AGAINST EVERYBODY: A DETROIT LOVE TALE 2

I can't lie and say I wasn't having fun with her. I guess I could get use to this. Having her around wasn't as bad as I liked it to be. I was fishing for any reason to complain about her because I was low key jealous of the bond her and Storm was forming.

When Empire went off, a breaking news story by FOX came on. What grabbed my attention was that they were filming right outside of The Crazy Horse.

"Reporting live from the west side of Detroit at the Crazy Horse gentleman's club, where there seems to have been an apparent homicide. We're still unclear of what actually happened here, but sources have told us that exotic dancer, LaToya 'Genie' Harris was given what people are calling a bad bag of coke. Apparently the mother of two snorted rat poisoning that was portrayed to be cocaine..."

Everything else she said was like 'blah blah' to me. Genie was dead.

I looked over at Storm, and she back at me. We both knew who was responsible for what happened. Hell, Carla knew too. The only person Genie copped from was Vice. I turned the TV off and took a big sip from my cup.

115

"Do he know something I don't," I asked Storm while shaking my head.

She shrugged her shoulder, "Shit, I don't know sis. You know he barely tells me anything."

Carla took a shot of the Effen, "Bitch, you dealing with a stone cold killer, that nigga gives no fuck."

Both me and Storm looked to Carla.

"Fuck you mean? What are you even talking about? Shut yo ass up. Talking that shit. Who do you think we're even talking about," I asked with an attitude.

Carla is an outsider – in my eyes at least. We don't know if she's a snitch or not. I cursed myself for even asking Storm about that shit. Damn.

"Jai chill. Carla is alright."

Carla laughed, "I swear, Jai, I'm getting sick of you. You always running your dick suckers!"

I just laughed. Yeah, the bitch could think shit was sweet if she wanted to. If anything came up about suspects and informants I'll know exactly who to place the blame on. I'd murk her ass myself. Vice looked out for me. I know he did. He knew something I didn't.

"I need to talk to him," I said as I reached for Storm's purse.

US AGAINST EVERYBODY: A DETROIT LOVE TALE 2

She smacked my hand away, "Okay bitch, but not over the phone. Are you nuts?"

I laughed, "No, ho, I'm drunk."

And that I was. Drunk as hell. But I felt loved though, on the real. Vice never really paid me any attention before Storm. I was like one of the groupie bitches begging for his attention, before. At first I wanted to suck and fuck him. But as soon as he showed interest in my best friend, those feelings went right out the window. Now I looked at him as a big brother. And apparently he considered me family as well.

[SEVEN]

Vice

Roadblocks. That's all I've been hitting for the past three weeks. I knew B worked for Oozy but I never saw him over there. What I wanted to do was run up on them pussy niggas and murk 'em all but I had to be smart. I had to make the right decision. I had to catch them with their guards down. And by the look of things, the niggas never let their guards now. They were always on top of shit.

I sat in my unmarked old school Chevy burning one with Reek. We were posted outside of the apartment building Oozy was always at. It had to be his main spot, where the most dough came from. I was waiting on B to touch down, as usual.

"I think that nigga skipped town," said Reek sounding choked up from the loud we were smoking.

I didn't say anything. I kept my eyes on the building. By now I knew all of his clientele. I knew what time they copped. I knew what time the drugs were dropped off. I knew just about everything about his organization. But

US AGAINST EVERYBODY: A DETROIT LOVE TALE 2

the niggas were thorough. Everything was careful. But to a dealing nigga like me, I knew what was up. The FEDS wouldn't know. But I knew.

I took a pull from the blunt and passed it to Reek before hopping out. He called out to me but I kept walking. A nigga was tired of waiting. These niggas ran deep but I didn't give a fuck. I was trying to tie up loose ends. Honestly, I was sick and tired of the shit popping off in the hood. The law was keeping a close watch because of the high murder rate on the seven and I didn't need that shit. I needed this beef, or whatever the fuck is was, squashed. If I couldn't catch the nigga B, Oozy was going to bring the nigga to me. Point blank period. I couldn't give a fuck less about how he might feel about it. Business is business and this shit chea, is fucking up my mental.

A nigga couldn't sleep at night. I wanted Branden bad as fuck. Every time I closed my eyes, I envisioned murdering him. I had to find him. I had to get my hands on him. No matter what I did, every single thought consisted of killing dude. I've never been the gory type of cat but that nigga...he deserved torture.

119

I heard the car door slam so I knew Reek was behind me.

"Yo," he said above a whisper.

I looked over my shoulder and said, "Fuck you whispering for nigga?!"

He was acting like more of a bitch than Dawson was the other time we came through here. Oozy really made these niggas nervous. I couldn't give a fuck less about a nigga's rep. I'm sure the fuck nigga heard about me too.

Reek jogged to catch up with me, "I just got out of the 'spital not to long ago. I ain't tryna go back no time soon, cuz."

I looked him up and down, "Fuck you come for then?" I waved him off, "Go sit in the whip, pussy."

I laughed but he didn't find shit funny.

"Man, you bugging." He shook his head, "Right or wrong, I'm riding with you though bro. Fuck!"

"You don't have to my nigga. You know I'm good with or without a squad," I seriously replied.

I was on some hot shit. Rolling up on these niggas without a plan. I could've been walking in on an ambush. Thing is though, I just didn't give a fuck. I needed to put a nigga six feet deep. If I did that, then I'd be burying at least one of my problems. Feel me?

US AGAINST EVERYBODY: A DETROIT LOVE TALE 2

I entered the parking lot, and just like before, the dudes posted up outside went for their burners. Fuck they thought? They were the only one's packing? I showed mine as well. Reek held his burner up and said everything was cool. I looked at him and shook my head. I didn't like the fact that the niggas I rolled through here with showed these dudes weakness. I didn't need any weak mothafuckas on my squad. Why is it that I'm the only one with heart enough to go to war with these niggas?

I walked up to the entrance and before I could open the door, someone else did. Some lil' bum ass nigga packing an AK-47. Off bat, Reek aimed the pistol at his dome. These niggas really thought they were the only ones out here with burners though.

"You got some kind of bidness over here," he asked while looking me up and down.

I pushed him aside and walked through.

"Obviously, fuck nigga. Gun packing for no reason. Knowing fuck well you ain't really bout that life!" I yelled over my shoulder as he brought the gun up aiming it at me.

121

"Let 'em up," I heard Oozy say.

"What up, Ooz! Teach these young niggas some manners. Raising a gun on a God. Don't he know that's sinning?"

Oozy waved me off and walked away as I gave home boy an ice cold stare. Reek tapped me on the shoulder to pull me out of my trance. Fuck boy didn't know how close he was to meeting his maker.

We walked away, heading to Oozy's apartment. Reek and Dawson might be worried about these boys but they bleed just like the next nigga. I fear no man, but God.

Oozy stood in his doorway, ducking a little because he was just too fucking tall. He waved his hands as to say we could come in. He told Reek to shut the door behind him. Oozy told us we could have a seat on the couch. He kept his eyes on Reek the entire time he spoke.

"No need for the heat, my man's," said Oozy as he lit a blunt. "Ain't nobody spilling blood over here, feel me?"

Reek looked at me and I nodded. Oozy is a laid back dude. He's more of a business cat. He don't strike me as the type of man that'll start a territory war.

I intertwined my fingers and rested my elbows on my knees as I spoke to him, "So, where's B?"

Oozy took a pull from his blunt and asked, "Who?"

US AGAINST EVERYBODY: A DETROIT LOVE TALE 2

I laughed, "Come on now, my nigga. Don't play me like a dummy."

He sat back on the couch and said, "Do I look like the type of man who plays?"

He didn't.

"Branden. Do you know him?"

Oozy nodded, "Yeah. I know the nigga by Branden. We don't call him anything but it. Ay," he choked from the blunt a little. "What's the issue? I would hate to have to make this friendship into something different. But if you keep coming around here on some animal shit, I just might have to. Feel me? You a young hot headed nigga. The type of niggas I don't spend too much time on anymore."

I should've felt insulted right? But I didn't. I felt where he was coming from. From his perspective I was becoming a problem he didn't need. I would've been on the same tip. Only difference is, I probably would've bodied him a long time ago. That goes back to what he just said. I'm a young hot headed nigga. Point, blank, period.

"Who is he to you? You give a fuck about him?"

"I don't give a fuck about anybody but Oozy," he offered me the blunt and I declined. He waved me off and continued, "I'm trying to learn you something. These niggas out here can't be trusted for real. At the end of the day all they really give a fuck about is themselves. Ain't no loyalty for real in this game." He looked at Reek as he spoke. "Loyalty is a rarity. Peep game, aight?"

He was spitting some real shit to me once again. I liked the nigga. He was trill. He spoke like a dude who knew what the fuck he was talking about. He lived this life. Back in the day young niggas looked up to him and the squad he use to run with. Speaking of such…

"What happened to Hustle Hard? That seems like a whole different generation of niggas out there."

"The same thing that happens to most drug cartels. Niggas get greedy and make hasty, dumb decisions and everything falls apart." He dumped some ashes out, "Only real niggas remain. *Hustle Hard* died years ago."

I waved him off, "Aight, whatever dog. Where B? Niggas been posted up on my blocks trying to set up shop." I frowned, "Yo call?"

"I told you. I don't do unnecessary beef. That's that nigga. What I need to expand for when I have a whole city to myself?" Oozy leaned over and scribbled something on a torn off sheet of paper, "What I don't like

US AGAINST EVERYBODY: A DETROIT LOVE TALE 2

is stupid niggas causing problems in my smooth operation." He handed me the paper, "That's his address. Take the problem directly to him. Give him a bullet from me to eat too."

Oozy sat back on the couch and finished off his blunt after telling us to 'get the fuck out'. I just laughed and slapped hands with him. True ass OG. I could respect it. As long as he wasn't trying to step on my toes, shit was gravy.

*

"Wassup, brown skin. Let me ask you something real quick," I said as I sat behind the wheel of my whip, posted up in front of the crib Oozy sent me to, talking to Storm on the hitter.

"What is it, sexy daddy?"

I laughed, "Did you introduce B to the family?"

She sucked her teeth, "Hell naw. Why?"

"I was just wondering, beautiful. I'll be there in a couple hours, aight? I'm handling a couple things."

"Okay. I love you. Be careful, Vice."

"Always. Love you too, lil mama."

I hung up.

If Storm didn't introduce B to Mack, why were they on the porch chopping it up?

US AGAINST EVERYBODY: A DETROIT LOVE
TALE 2

[EIGHT]

Storm

"**W**ait, what," I yelled into the phone as I hurriedly grabbed my yoga pants out of my overnight bag.

"Your father…he's in the hospital Storm!"

My momma was crying into the phone. What she just told me before saying my dad was in the hospital was barely audible. Apparently there had been some type of shootout. My momma was going on and on about how Vice was responsible. I hung up on her and called him but for some reason he wasn't answering.

It was after three in the morning and we were still at Jai's crib. My heart was pounding nearly out of my chest. Once again, it felt like I was being pulled in two different

127

directions. My heart was telling me that Vice would never hurt me in the way my momma was saying. I didn't even know what condition my dad was in, nor if Vice was really responsible.

I shimmied as I pulled my yoga pants up. I flicked the on the lamp and almost had a heart attack at the sight before me. Jai was sitting in the corner, knees to her chest, rocking back and forth with her eyes bucked.

"Sis! What the hell?!"

"I...I can't sleep. I," she wiped sweat from her brow and said, "I need something, Storm."

She lowered her head out of embarrassment. Too much shit was going on. How am I supposed to be here for her when I have a family emergency? I walked over to her and kneeled next to her. I grabbed her body and pulled her closer to me. I knew she needed the drugs but she'd just have to do without.

"Be strong, Jai. Please. I can't deal with this right now."

She jerked away from me and I tumbled back a little, "How in the fuck am I supposed to be strong Storm? Huh!? How!? When all I can think about is snorting a fucking line?! I can't sleep because my mind is racing! I can't do this!"

She stood up and went for the front door. I jumped up and rushed to her. I wrapped my arms around her body

US AGAINST EVERYBODY: A DETROIT LOVE TALE 2

and pulled her back. When I pulled her, we stumbled over Carla who was sprawled out on the floor. We fell on top of her and she let out a loud grunt.

Jai rolled right over Carla and ran for the door again. I got up as fast as I could. But before I could get to her, she was out of the door. Instead of running after her, I cried. Because too much shit was going on. Trying to deal with it all was stressful.

"What the hell is going on," asked Carla as she held onto her back, which I assume was hurting pretty badly since we had fallen directly on her.

I wiped my face and closed the screen door. She was running down the street in the direction of Vice's dope spot. I grabbed my designer bag and car keys before finally addressing Carla who was limping around the living room.

"She's feigning. Mack is in the hospital. My mom is saying Vice is the reason," I shook my head as I slipped my UGGs on. "I have too much going on right now, Carla. I'm trying to be strong but I just can't."

I broke down crying and Carla limped over and wrapped her arms around me.

"Shhh, Don't cry sweetie. You go see what's going on at the hospital and I'll take care of Jai. I know where she's headed."

I knew Jai would feel some type of way about Carla being in her business but at that moment I didn't give a damn. There was no way in hell I'd be able to handle all of this alone.

I thanked Carla repeatedly before telling her I'd be right back as soon as possible. She was very understanding. She told me to take my time and to not worry about hurrying up back there.

I nodded and ran out of the door, with my phone glued to my ear calling Vice once again.

*

I cursed as I hung up after calling him three more times before I finally made it to the hospital. I parked, grabbed my purse, and jetted into the hospital.

I walked up to the receptionists and a lightbulb went off in my head.

"Hi. I'm here to see Vice Williams."

US AGAINST EVERYBODY: A DETROIT LOVE TALE 2

It's worth a shot right? Vice always answers his phone for me. Busy or not. So him not answering for nearly an hour raised all kinds of red flags.

My heart beat pitter-pattered rapidly against my chest as she typed his name into the keyboard. I impatiently tapped my fingernails on the counter, praying to God that he's not here. Hoping like heck that he's at home knocked out sleep. Begging God that what my mom said happened isn't true.

My heart sank when she said, "I'm sorry, there's no Vice here."

My mind was elsewhere when I nodded and asked for a pass to see Derek Hamilton. I couldn't even recollect where she told me to go. I walked away, blinded. My emotions everywhere.

I was so out of it that I didn't hear my mom calling out for me and she was standing directly in my face. I didn't realize what was happening until I ran right into her.

She grabbed and held me, with tears falling from her eyes. I cried too, and as much as I didn't like to admit,

131

they were for Vice. A part of me was sad for my dad as well, but I was really worried about Vice. More so because I didn't know where he was and had no way of finding him. As we walked to Mack's room, my mom filled me in on everything. He was only hit in the leg. He was doing fine and trying to leave already.

I couldn't understand for the life of me, why my mom was acting like he was dying when we talked earlier. And she's still crying. For what? The man is okay. In all of my years, I've been close to my father. But we're nowhere near as close as we use to be. We don't even talk anymore. I can't say that I'm really heartbroken about it. I'm a grown woman and he wasn't ready to let go and let me make my own decisions. He was treating me like a high schooler, forbidding me to see someone. Crazy ass man. So whatever. I've distanced myself from him.

I walked in the room and he immediately frowned his face up at me. I shook my head and turned to leave but my mother blocked the doorway.

"Not now! This is when we come together," she yelled as she pointed to a chair next to his bed.

I sucked my teeth and went over to take a seat. My dad looked down at me with dismay. Disgust and disappointment was written all over his face.

I swallowed my pride and said, "Hey old man."

US AGAINST EVERYBODY: A DETROIT LOVE TALE 2

He didn't say anything. All he did was shake his head and sip from his cup. I threw my hands up and began to stand.

"Sit yo ass down, Storm," yelled Mack in a voice so booming he frightened me more than he ever had.

I flinched and sat back down with tears in my eyes.

He pointed his finger at me as he spoke, "You see this shit? You think that nigga gives a fuck about you? He sent some bullets my way. Gave zero fucks about your feelings. I told yo young, hot and ready ass that you were just his flavor of the month! Look at this yo! He could've killed me but I'm too much of an OG! Weak niggas came for me but couldn't take me out. Thank God, right? You wouldn't even be talking to me right now," he slammed his fist down on his side table. "War is on! And if you have half a mind you'll stay the fuck away from him! Damn what is it going to take? He was responsible for your sister being in the hospital, now he pulled the trigger himself to get me in this bitch. You gotta be a dumb ass—

"Watch yo mouth, old head. Keep it a hunnet my nigga!"

I looked up and Vice was standing there in a black wifebeater with a bandage on his shoulder. It took everything to stop me from running to his side. Where had he been all night? The nurses and my mother was trying to keep him away from the room. Despite the people holding him back, he overpowered them.

He smiled at me, "Wassup brown skin."

My heart fluttered and I stood. But it was beyond my control. I was attracted to him. Like a negative to a positive. We were magnetics, simply doing what magnetics do. Attracting to one another.

Mack yelled, "STORM!"

I sat back down and buried my face in my hands. I heard so much commotion, but through it all, I heard Vice's voice.

"Tell her why I did what I did my nigga! Keep that shit G! You supposed to be an OG right?! Keep that shit G then fuck nigga!"

Vice was trying to get at my daddy. My mom was going crazy, as were the nurses trying to calm everything down.

I took my hands from my face and looked at my daddy. He was looking back at me with pain in his eyes. He was furious as well, but in that moment, as he looked at me he was sad. I leaned over his bed and asked him what Vice was talking about.

US AGAINST EVERYBODY: A DETROIT LOVE TALE 2

He shook his head and tightly closed his eyes, trying to fight back tears I suppose.

"I didn't mean for things to go as badly as they did, Storm. Forgive me. I was just trying to teach you a lesson. That's all!"

I stood up, "Daddy, what are u talking about?" I asked him through clenched teeth.

He was silent. So Vice intervened, "Tell her fuck nigga! Explain to your daughter how you had The Crazy Horse shot up, knowing she was there! Tell her, bitch! Tell her how you had B, rest his ho ass soul, do it!"

My heart sunk into my chest and I felt faint, "Wha-what? Daddy please tell me he's lying!"

"Derek! How could you! How could you!?"

If there was anybody in the room who knew my daddy, it was my mom. She knew it was true, so I did too. She was beating him in the chest. I heard one of the nurses tell a coworker to call security. I was stuck. I couldn't move. It felt like I was in quicksand. Life as I once knew it was over.

"Baby girl! Please forgive me," said Mack reaching out to me as Vice pulled me into his chest.

"I told you, brown skin, I'll cause havoc out here for you. No one is exempt. The only reason I didn't kill him is because I wanted you to see for yourself how much of a piece of shit he is," whispered Vice into my ear as he tried to lead me out of the room.

I wiped tears from my face and stopped him, "I need to stay with my mom right now, okay? This is a lot for me to take in. I'll come see you later."

"I'll be at the crib. Waiting on you, aight? Just come through when you're ready, lil mama." He kissed me on the forehead and gave me a comforting smile before leaving the room.

By then, security was there with DPD. I watched as stress washed over Vice's face. One of the detectives came into the room with us and the other grabbed Vice's arm and went in the other direction. The room was slowly but surely clearing out. My mom was still pretty messed up but that didn't stop her from cursing the detective out and telling him to leave.

He nodded and put his card on the table before leaving the room.

I ignored Mack as he called out, begging for my forgiveness, and hugged my mom. She sobbed uncontrollably on my shoulder as she apologized for

US AGAINST EVERYBODY: A DETROIT LOVE TALE 2

everything I've gone through. I looked over her shoulder at Mack with a scowl on my face. I couldn't believe he did that. I couldn't believe he was responsible for Jai being hit. He actually sat back and blamed it all on Vice. He actually had me believing it was some random act of violence against Vice. He wanted us a part so bad that he really risked me being hit. I was truly hurt.

"I knew you'd be okay, Storm—

I cut him off, "How could you know!? Bullets don't have names, Mack! You can save your bull shit ass apology. You're not sorry for what you did; you're only sorry because I found out!"

I let go of my mom and made my way out of the room. My momma grabbed my hand and we walked out together. She was hurt more than I was, which I could definitely understand. Her ex-husband and father of her child sent someone to shoot up a club he knew her daughter and friends would be at. All because I was seeing Vice. And not to mention, he got Branden to do it. My dad didn't know I was even seeing B. Not to my knowledge at least. I don't even know how they know each other.

We walked out of the hospital and to the parking garage where we sat inside of my car in silence. Momma laid her head on my shoulder as she gave my hand a squeeze every now and then.

"I'm so sorry, sweetie," she apologized for the fiftieth time.

I kissed her on the cheek, "You don't have to keep apologizing, ma. It's not your fault."

"It is my fault. It's my responsibility to make sure you're taken care of. I—

"Stop blaming yourself. It's not your fault. Only one to blame is my da... I mean Mack."

He's lost all respect from me. I don't care about what anyone thinks. He really put me harm's way. A man who's protected me my whole life. Hell, now I need protecting from him.

My phone rung, *Carla*. I sighed loudly. I prayed to God she had some good news for me. I couldn't handle anymore bullshit.

"Yeah," I answered.

"I can't find Jai. I went to the spot but she wasn—

I rolled my eyes and interrupted her, "I'll be there in about an hour, Carla. This bit—I mean...man I'll be there okay?"

US AGAINST EVERYBODY: A DETROIT LOVE TALE 2

My voice cracked as I spoke. I was trying to be strong, when being strong was the furthest thing from my mind. I wanted to break down. I wanted to lie in bed, bury my face in my pillow and let out a gut wrenching scream.

"Storm, are you o—

"I'm okay, Carla. I…I'll be there shortly."

I hung up and literally threw my phone against the windshield. I prayed my anger didn't cause me to break my only way of communication right now.

"What's going on, Stormy," asked my momma.

I lied my head on the steering wheel, "I'll talk to you about it later, okay?"

She rubbed my back, "Baby, you need to go home and ge—

I yelled, "I can't go home! My best friend is somewhere in the streets feigning for a hit of cocaine! Okay?! I have to take care of Jai! As usual! If I don't, who will!? Definitely not Ryan because she's not smart enough to keep a good man!"

139

I was lashing out. I didn't want to, but got damn! Can a bitch get a break?

"Aw, Storm, baby," she rubbed my back, "I can—

"Just go ma. Please...I just need to be alone right now."

She kissed me on the cheek before telling me she loved me and getting out of the car.

I sat there crying for a good twenty minutes before cranking the engine up and pulling off.

US AGAINST EVERYBODY: A DETROIT LOVE
TALE 2

[NINE]
Jai

If this is what rock bottom felt like, then I'd definitely hit it. It wasn't my fault though. I blame Vice and his flunkies. He wouldn't let them sell me any coke.

I had just left the spot, after being rejected. As I was on my way walking around the corner back to my house some guy pulled up on side of me. At first he was trying to flirt but I guess he saw my obvious need of drugs and tried a different approach.

"What you looking for sexy," he asked.

I kept on walking as I replied, "I need to get high."

"Say, I got some loud. We can chief, baby girl."

I glanced at him and chuckled, "I have my own weed."

"Ooooh, you have a taste for something else huh,"

I rubbed my arms in an attempt to warm them up, "Yes…"

He stopped at a red light and dangled a bag of powder out of the window.

"What's that," I excitedly asked.

"Crack cocaine baby."

I stood there. Frozen. *Coke snorting bitch now, crack head in a few months…* Cinnamon's voice echoed through my mind as I thought about the last thing she said to me. I was tripping. I wanted to take that crack so bad but I knew better. My mouth salivated at the thought of being high. I knew I shouldn't. I knew it was the absolute worst thing to do. If I knew that, then why was I slowly walking towards the car?

I was being pulled. My mind knew I didn't need to be doing no fucking crack, but my body was urging for it. I needed it. It wasn't coke but it'd do right?

Just as quickly as I was grabbing the bag from him, it was knocked out of my hand. I looked up and tears filled my eyes as I looked into the face of my daddy. I shook my head, and the hallucination went away. Who stood before me was Ryan. He gawked down on me in disgust.

US AGAINST EVERYBODY: A DETROIT LOVE TALE 2

"Get the fuck on," he yelled to the man.

He scurried off and Ryan held onto my body, shaking me, "What is wrong with you, Jai? Huh!? What is wrong with you!?"

I didn't say anything, as tears poured down my face.

What was he doing over here?

"What....why are you here," I managed to ask.

He grabbed my hand and led me to his car, which was parked at a pump at the gas station.

"I'm no stranger to addiction. I noticed how you were feigning earlier. So, I knew you were going to try something stupid, Jai. I've been posted outside of your house for hours," said Ryan as he put me in his car and strapped my seatbelt on.

I sat there embarrassed with tears rolling down my face. I never wanted this addiction to get this bad. Never in my life did I fathom I'd be in this predicament. I buried my face in my palms and cried. I didn't want Ryan to see me so weak.

He got in the car and removed my hands from my face. He frowned up at me, and threw a bottle of water in my lap.

"Your lips are dry," he said before pulling off.

As badly as I wanted to pull the sun visor down and look at my reflection, I couldn't bring myself to do so. I knew I looked bad. I knew how stupid I looked. I was outside in forty degree weather in a tank, booty shorts, and some UGG boots. All night, I sat in that corner fighting with myself. I was doing a pretty good job until Storm cut the light on. I couldn't control the urge anymore. So I jetted the fuck up.

I cracked the bottle open and drank it down in one sitting. I was thirsty.

Ryan glanced at me as he turned on seven mile. I looked out of the window to avoid eye contact. I couldn't stop my leg from bouncing. , he placed his hand on my knee and it stopped. I turned towards him but he kept his eyes on the road.

"Thank you, Ryan. I don't know what I would've done I—

"You know exactly what you would've done if I didn't stop it from happen," said Ryan interrupting me.

I nodded and said, "Well, yeah, you're right. I do know. But I do appr—

US AGAINST EVERYBODY: A DETROIT LOVE
TALE 2

"Don't mention it. Ain't no thang."

He was upset and I was embarrassed as hell! How did this happen to me?! Got damn! My life had done a complete one eighty. I sat there, silently crying as he rubbed my leg.

"Stop crying, Jai."

I was deep in my thoughts. Thinking of how upset my daddy is with me right now. Hell, my mother too. Although I didn't get to meet her, she died for me in a sense. I should be better. The way my daddy talked about her was like she was a businesswoman. Professional, classy, a diva. I have the last two down pack. I guess you can say I'm a professional in a way too. I'm a pro at getting what I want out of men but that's nothing to brag about. She was a college graduate with her head screwed on tight. Her and my dad was married before they even had sex. Now look at her daughter. A damn stripping, drugged out, whore.

I sniffled as I silently cried, trying to hide my tears from Ryan. I wiped my face and looked over at him. He's a good man. I'm no good for him. All a bitch like me will do is drag him down. I snatched my seatbelt off and opened the car door to jump out.

Ryan smashed down on the breaks in the middle of the freeway, and pulled my arm as I hung half way out of the car. Thank God it was four in the morning, and there was little to no traffic. He pulled me so hard that I went crashing against his chest. Ryan grabbed the sides of my head and screamed in my face.

"What the fuck is wrong with you girl, huh!? What the fuck are you trying to do!? Kill yourself, Jai!? What is wrong with you damnit!"

He shook my head as he spoke. I tried to back away from him but his grip was very forceful.

"I'm just a burden to you," I yelled through my sobs.

Ryan let me go, reached over, and slammed the door. He scowled in my face as he strapped my seatbelt on again. He sat back on his seat, resting his head on the headrest before hitting the locks.

"Jai, understand when someone is trying to help you. I shouldn't be but I can't watch you self-destruct the way you are," said Ryan as he began to slowly pull off.

I pulled my knees up to my chest and tried to ignore the yearning for coke.

"All I need is one li—

US AGAINST EVERYBODY: A DETROIT LOVE TALE 2

"Don't sit there and ask me for no fuckin' coke, Jai! Just shut the fuck up and enjoy the ride aight," yelled Ryan as he scratched his head.

I was stressing him out and I didn't want to do that. That's why I tried to leave. I don't want to be a burden to anybody. I'm not his problem. He broke up with me. Why was he even in my hood? He should've been on campus. He has class today.

"Ryan...you have class in a coupl—

"I'm not going. Please, Jai, just...just let me think alright?"

He wanted me to be quiet, and quiet is what I struggled to be for the rest of the ride to his place.

*

I lowered my body into the warm bubble bath Ryan prepared for me as soon as we hit the door. He sat on side of the tub, leaving someone a voicemail about how he wasn't going to be available today. When I asked him who it was, he told me he was scheduled to meet with a

147

scout for the Green Bay Packers at ten. I felt horrible. I told him he needed to call back and tell them he was able to meet. He shook his head and told me he wasn't going to let me go cold turkey alone.

Ryan offered to pay for me to go to rehab at a nice facility but I declined. I didn't want him spending any more money. Trust, a bitch could appreciate some cash. But I didn't want him thinking I liked him just because of that. In the beginning that's exactly what I wanted. Now things are different. I've never met a man as caring as he was. I've never had a man show interest in anything but sex. But Ryan cared. Although he made it perfectly clear to me that we weren't a couple and he was only doing this out of the kindness of his heart. Yeah, he was talking all of that now but just wait and see what happens once I get this damn monkey off my back.

I tried my best to relax and ease my mind but no matter what, the craving for cocaine took over. My body went into tremors and Ryan sat on side of the tub rubbing my back the whole time. He was trying everything to help. He had soothing music playing from his sound bar. He was even on Google searching ways to go 'cold turkey'. One suggestion in particular made him uneasy.

"How much did you use," asked Ryan.

I opened my eyes and struggled to say, "Only…only a little over a gram…gram a week."

He nodded and stood up, "I'll…I'll be back."

US AGAINST EVERYBODY: A DETROIT LOVE TALE 2

I hugged onto the tub and pleaded, "Please don't leave me."

"I'm only going to the closet Jai," said Ryan as he turned to leave.

"You... You have coke here?"

He nodded and walked out of the room.

Ryan didn't strike me as a drug dealer, but I guess you learn something new every day. I had so many questions for him. Like, why was he letting me feign knowing damn well he had some fucking dope! Just like that, my mood had changed. I was pissed. I couldn't believe he was letting me feign like this and he could've given me a bag. Shit, I would've paid for the shit. It's nothing.

As soon as he came back in the bathroom I cut right into him.

"Really, Ryan?! You sell dope!? And yo couldn't let me cop up off of you!"

He looked at me like I was crazy, "You think I sell dope? And even if I did, you really think I would've given you any?"

He waved me off as turned and he poured the coke on the bathroom counter. My mouth salivated at the sight.

"Well what the fuck are you doing with coke, Ryan!?"

He looked at me over his shoulder and said, "It was mine."

US AGAINST EVERYBODY: A DETROIT LOVE
TALE 2

[TEN]

Vice

They couldn't wait to question a nigga. Thing is, I had no words for them. I chose to remain silent. Fuck ass cops followed me out of the hospital talking all kinds of shit. They accused me of shooting Mack and killing B, which I of course am guilty of. I went fucking crazy when I saw Mack and B shooting the shit like they were good ol' friends. Especially since wifey said she hadn't even introduced them.

The detectives continued to follow me to the car bombarding me with questions. I walked on side of them, not paying them any mind as I reflected on what happened a couple hours ago.

As soon as I ended the phone conversation with Storm, I grabbed the Glock from under my seat and hopped out. Reek was right there with me, hand on the pistol as we walked up to what appeared to be a trap house. Mack, being the OG he claimed to be, went for his heat too. B tried to run away into the crib but I crippled him. Sent a bullet ripping right through his spinal cord. He fell down the stairs as soon as the bullet came in contact with him.

I stepped over his crying ass and mobbed up the stairs. By then, Mack was in the crib. He knew I was on some animal shit and there was nothing stopping me. Not even the semi-automatic bullet that Mack sent ripping through my shoulder. Reek let off a single shot that hit Mack in the leg. I told bro not to kill him. I wanted to know what was what.

I grunted in pain as I gawked down at Mack who was reaching for his gat that I kicked away.

He spit at me and I kicked him in the face.

"Pussy ass nigga," he yelled, "Take me out, boy! Do what yo wanna do!"

I laughed through my pain as I clenched my shoulder. I can't even sit and lie like the shit wasn't killing me, because it was. I kneeled down and said, "Yeah, taking you out is what I want to do. But I won't do that until you tell me why you kicking it with that nigga B."

US AGAINST EVERYBODY: A DETROIT LOVE TALE 2

'Nigga, fuck you," yelled Mack.

I nodded and walked out of the house. Luckily, B was still breathing. Barely hanging on though. I stood over him and aimed the gun at his head as I asked, "How you know that nigga?"

B coughed up some blood before responding, "I...I work for him on some...some low key shit. He's... He sent me on the six to set up shop," he coughed some more, "I don't have shit to do with the beef y'all got popping. The only reason I shot up the Crazy Horse was because he told me too."

Branden thought I was there for Mack. He had not a clue that the bullets in my glock had his name on them. Nigga laid there confessing to crimes like he got caught up in Mack's shit. When in reality, Mack got caught up in his. I did appreciate the confession though. That was just the confirmation I needed. Branden fessing up didn't mean a thing to me though. Sure in the fuck didn't stop me from sending a bullet ripping through his dome.

"Two bullets, my G. The one in the back was for Ooz, this one...this one to the dome, that's strictly from me, homie," I told him before pulling the trigger.

153

I walked back into the house and Reek was standing in front of Mack with the gun to his head.

"Ready for me to off this nigga, brodie?"

I ignored him and kneeled down in front of Mack who didn't appear to have a trace of fear in his eyes as he stared down the barrel of Reek's pistol.

I pressed my knee against his gunshot wound as I asked him, "That was you huh?"

"Fuck is you talking about," he asked as he turned in my direction.

I lightly pushed Reek's gun away from Mack's head and he backed up. I pressed my glock in the middle of his head, right between his eyes.

"The Crazy Horse," I placed my finger on the trigger, "Don't even fix yo mouth to lie, pussy nigga. Or I swear I'll give you a bullet to eat for dinner. B just told me everything."

Mack shook his head and yelled fuck.

"Keep it G for once in your life, old head," I told them through clinched teeth.

"Yeah but—

"If you knew I was at the horse, then you knew yo daughter was with me. Besides that, you knew Jai worked there right?"

US AGAINST EVERYBODY: A DETROIT LOVE TALE 2

"Man, I was just try—

I yelled, "Shut the fuck up bitch nigga!" I was itching to pull the trigger. I started to but then a thought came to mind.

If I kill this nigga and try to explain why to Storm it won't mean shit. She wouldn't believe that. Would you? I needed him to tell her herself. He was so busy trying to keep her away from me that all he did with that stupid ass stunt was bring us closer together. She'll never forgive the fuck nigga. What type of nigga put's his daughter in danger?

I looked to Reek and told him to call an ambulance. He gave me a confused look and I told him I'd explain later.

I lowered the gun and sent a bullet ripping into the same spot Reek shot him in before. He let out a loud, echoic cry.

I pressed the barrel of the glock into his wound. Not giving a fuck about the blood, or meat getting my gun messy.

155

"Listen to me, fuck boy. What you're going to do is go to the hospital, get Storm up there and tell her the truth," he started to refuse and I yelled in his face, *"And if you don't imma come see you. I swear on my dead momma. Next time I won't have a reason to spare your life. Be the real nigga you always claim to be for once in your life."*

I heard sirens and knew that it was time to go. We ran out the crib and into the whip where I hurriedly drove off.

"I have an eye witness for real this time Vice," said Detective Olivia, pulling me out of my trance.

I nodded and smiled at her. Bitch thought I was supposed to be shook just because she claimed she had a witness. All I'll do is find out who and simply off the rat. Just like before. Shouldn't these pussy ass cops get it by now? They can't touch me.

"If that's true, Olivia, why aren't I in cuffs," I asked as I got inside of my lac.

She smile sweetly, "I'll see you soon."

"Keep coming around smiling and harassing a nigga, I'ma give you this dick," I started the whip. "That's what you want ain't it, bitch?"

Her cheeks turned red and she frowned up. She looked over her shoulder for her partner who was several feet behind.

US AGAINST EVERYBODY: A DETROIT LOVE TALE 2

Detective Olivia leaned in my window and said, "No you piece of shit but I know a few fellas in Jackson who will have a field day on your fine ass!"

I smiled and rubbed my face, "A nigga is fine as fuck huh?"

I winked and sped off, only missing her toes by a couple inches.

*

Fifteen minutes later I was pulling into my garage, yawning and rubbing my eyes. Tonight had been very eventful. After everything popped off with them niggas, I had to clean up. Storm was blowing my phone up like crazy but I was so pissed that I didn't want to talk to her. Not because I was pissed at her but I was afraid that I'd tell her what I found out before Mack could. In a way, I still did that. But shit, he wasn't going to. I'm glad I went with my gut feeling. I knew the nigga was a straight up bitch. Besides that, what man wants to tell his daughter he had her shot at? So I went up to the hospital. He wasn't going to tell her.

157

Now I'm sitting in the whip, having a hard time getting out. A nigga is dead ass tired. I grabbed my phone from my pocket and scrolled down to her name. I needed to see if she was good. What she just found out wasn't no petty shit. A nigga she's loved her whole life turned out to be on some fuck shit. Storm was close to her pops before I came into the picture. I won't even blame myself for that. Hell, it's his fault he couldn't accept the fact that his daughter was falling for a G.

I hit the dial button and waited.

"Hello," answered Storm sounding like she had the weight of the world on her shoulders.

"You aight lil' mama," I asked as I got out of the car.

She sighed, "The furthest thing from it. I just want to sleep."

"Come through, let a nigga hold you."

I heard her smile through her voice, "I'm looking for—wait hold up someone's beeping on the other line."

I unlocked the door and walked in the crib. First thing I did was kick my shoes off and head to the bathroom. My shoulder was hurting like fuck. I had to do what I didn't have time to do earlier. I grabbed some alcohol, a knife, my lighter, and some towels before I stood at the bathroom sink. I took the bandage off and stared at the ugly wound.

US AGAINST EVERYBODY: A DETROIT LOVE TALE 2

I pressed the phone against my ear with my good shoulder as I opened the bottle of alcohol.

"Ahhh, fuck," I yelled as I poured the alcohol on it.

"Hello, Vice? You okay," yelled Storm returning to our call.

"Ye—yeah shorty. What it is?"

"That was Jai," she sighed, "I don't even want to get into that drama right now. Is that invitation still valid?"

I smiled as I grabbed my shoulder and tied a shirt around it, "Fa sho, brown skin, always."

"Yessss. I'm on my way."

"Aight."

I sat the phone down when we hung up. I flicked my lighter, holding the flame to the knife. Once it was hot enough, I forced myself to insert it into the gunshot wound, fishing for the bullet. I bit down on the other end of the shirt tied to my arm, to soothe my pain. After digging for a few seconds, I found it and it fell into the sink. I quickly untied the shirt and applied pressure to the

159

wound to stop the bleeding. I beat on the sink out of frustration. The shit hurt like hell. Probably worse than being shot. Once the bleeding was under control, I cleaned it again and stitched it up with needle and thread from my sewing kit I had for emergencies just like this.

Twenty minutes later, as I laid on the couch, I heard keys jiggling at my door. I stood up and walked to the door. When she finally unlocked it, and walked in, I grabbed her. Despite the pain in my shoulder, I lifted Storm from her feet and held her tightly. Lil mama was fucked up. The tears wetting my bare chest up told me so.

I cradled her as we walked to my room. I laid her on the bed and removed her ugly ass UGG boots, and then her socks. I left her yoga pants on. She didn't like to be without them when she was on her period if we slept together. I take notice to a lot of shit. She removed her tank and laid back on the pillow in her bra. I stood there, looking down at her. Even with puffy eyes, and in a bonnet she was beautiful.

Storm held her arms open for me and I joined her in bed. Shorty made me feel in ways I really didn't like. I've never been this open with anybody. I didn't like it. I wore my heart on my sleeve when it came to her. Thing is though, no matter how much I hated the shit, I couldn't help but have those feelings.

US AGAINST EVERYBODY: A DETROIT LOVE
TALE 2

I held her from the back, in a way that said I didn't want to ever lose her. And that was real shit. I buried my face in her neck, inhaling her womanly scent as she softly cried.

"I love you, Vice. More than I ever thought possible."

I didn't know how to really respond to that. I felt the same way but I couldn't come out and say any soft shit like that so I just told her I loved her too. We fell asleep just as daylight was peeking through.

*

Hours later, I had an eerie feeling. Like something was off. And when I opened my eyes, I knew just what. Standing next to my bed was a nigga in a mask, with an AK in my face. Off instinct, I turned around in search of Storm. She was gone.

"Get up nigga," said a familiar voice.

I smiled and stood up, "What you rocking a mask for, Tank? I know it's you."

161

He pressed the gun to my back and yelled, "Shut the fuck up."

I held my hands up, "First mistake you made was letting me wake up. Second is, you talking too much." I slightly looked over my shoulder at him, "You ain't really bout this life, Tank."

I was talking shit, alright. But low key, I was nervous as hell. I've never been caught this 'naked' in my entire life. I didn't have a pistol on me or shit. The closet gun was the one in my nightstand and he was blocking it. He had the drop on me. I can't even say I saw this coming. I definitely didn't. What I did to Lando happened damn near six months ago. It took him long enough right? Tank ain't a gangsta type nigga. He was nervous.

Where the fuck is Storm? I prayed she was in the bathroom or something. I hoped like hell he didn't have someone else with him who had her. I didn't even want to mention her because he probably didn't even know she was here.

He snatched his face mask off and wiped sweat off of his forehead before speaking, "Fuck you nigga! You…you deserve this! Lando didn't' deserve that shit yo!"

He was scared. Never killed a nigga a day in his life. I turned around and faced him. He held the gun with both hands as his body shook. If I wanted to, I could snatch the

US AGAINST EVERYBODY: A DETROIT LOVE TALE 2

gun right from his pussy ass. And that's what I decided to do.

But before I could get my hands on it, he fell to the floor. My eyebrows knitted together out of confusion. I looked down at him, wondering why there was blood leaking from the back of his head. When I looked up, I realized why.

Storm was standing there with a bloody frying pan in her hands, shaking. I stepped over Tank's unconscious body and grabbed her. Her eyes were bucked as she looked down at Tank.

"Brown skin," I called out to her. She didn't respond. I held the sides of her face, staring into her unblinking eyes, "Baby…You good. You straight." I reassured her.

"He was going to kill you. I—I don't want you to die, Vice," she said with a shaky voice.

I grabbed the back of her head and pulled her into my chest. Shorty is a rider. I appreciated the fuck up out of her for that. I knew Tank wasn't dead and that I'd have to finish him off, but she looked out fa sho. Storm was shaken up because she thought she killed him. I whispered in her ear that she hadn't. A sigh of relief escaped her mouth, and her body fell limp.

There was movement behind me. I looked out of the corner of my eye and Tank was slowly regaining consciousness. The AK was a few inches from him. I quickly reached into the nightstand, grabbed my burner, and blew the back of his head clean off, just as he was grabbing the AK. Storm let out a scream that sounded like it came from the pit of her soul. I grabbed her, covered her mouth, and shielded her eyes away from the gruesome scene.

We walked out of the bedroom and I sat her on the couch. I paced the living room floor as she sat there rocking back and forth with tears rolling down her face.

"Fuck! Brown skin, baby…" I said kneeling down in front of her, "I'm sorry you had to witness that shit." I brought her hands up to my lips and kissed her knuckles, "Look, I swear on everything you won't ever have to see anything like that again. Let me go clean this shit up and ge—

"No. Don't do that. Call 9-1-1 and tell them someone broke in the house."

"Man, baby, they ain't tryna he—

"I have a CCW. I'll tell them I killed him. It was self-defense. Simple as that. *I* had every right to kill him.

US AGAINST EVERYBODY: A DETROIT LOVE TALE 2

I'll get in some trouble but it'll be my first offense so I'll just get a slap on the wrist—"

I stood up, "Nah. Fuck naw! I'm not letting you ta—

Storm stood up and grabbed me, "You're not letting me do anything. I'm grown, Vice! This is my decision."

I yanked away from her and headed for the room to clean up. She was on my heels though. Storm was in my ear about calling 9-1-1 but I wasn't hearing that. I couldn't let her take the rap for some shit I did. That just ain't me. True, she'd get a slap on the wrist but I couldn't have that. Lil' mama is precious, golden, a fucking diamond. I won't let some shit I did tarnish her name. I can't have lil' mama out here with bad rep because of me.

She was quiet so I looked over my shoulder and caught her on the phone. Before I could snatch the phone out of her hand she was speaking.

"Yes! Someone broke into my home and I killed him. Oh my God, it's so much blood," yelled Storm into the phone as she sobbed loudly. It was over.

I sluggishly walked away and sat on the bed, staring down at Tank as I drug my hands down my face. I looked up at Storm and she was staring at me. I tore my eyes away from hers. I was pissed. I didn't want her to do that shit. Instead of listening, she did what the fuck she wanted to do. I stood up and punched a hole in the wall.

I wanted to shield her away from this side of me. Like I said, she's a fucking diamond! She don't need to be in this shit. I don't want to corrupt her, but I felt like I was doing just that. she asked me for the address and I ignored her. She loudly sucked her teeth and left the room, to get the address off the house I guess.

As I stood over Tank's dead body I wondered how he found out where I stood. There were only four people who knew where I was resting my head. Reek, Dawson, Storm, and Joslyn. Scratch Storm out. Shorty's official. Somebody was fucking with me. Unless the fuck nigga followed me here. My mind was on some other shit as I drove home. Usually, I kept my eyes on the rearview. Last night I didn't.

Storm came back into the room with her phone in her hands, and her lips drawn into her mouth.

"They're on th—

"Don't ever do that again. When I tell you I don't want you in the middle of something, respect it, aight brown skin?" I said as picked the frying pan up after

US AGAINST EVERYBODY: A DETROIT LOVE TALE 2

wiping my prints off the burner. I sat it on the nightstand and walked away, leaving her in the bedroom.

I expected her to stay there but instead, she followed me with the gun in her hands so that her prints would be on it. I shook my head. This was a side of her I've never seen. To be honest, the thorough shit turned me on. I still didn't need her to be involved in this life at all. I went to the kitchen, cleaned it off really well and put it with the other dishes. Throwing it out would've been suspicious since it came with a set. I had to be careful in case they decided to look around.

I left the kitchen and went to the bathroom with Storm still trailing behind me. I lifted the toilet seat, pulled my dick out and pissed like she wasn't standing in the room. She wasn't bothered by it a bit. Storm stood there with her arms folded over her chest, mean mugging me. I glance at her and shook my head.

"All I'm saying, lil mama, is that I don't want you involved in that lifestyle period."

"We're together. *You're* involved in that lifestyle. *I'm* involved in that lifestyle. Don't treat me like a baby, Vice. I knew what I was getting into when I agreed to get

167

back with you. And don't forget what you told me when we were fucking with ol' girl. *Your beef is my beef.* Period. I'm involved. Deal with it," said Storm before sitting the gun on the sink and walking out to answer the door.

I shook my dick and pulled my boxers up. As I stood at the sink washing my hands, I smiled. Shorty's a mothafuckin rider.

[ELEVEN]

Storm

They didn't even bother sending an ambulance. The coroner came, and right behind him were the police. I was a nervous wreck and I didn't even bother hiding it. Why would I? I'm supposed to be nervous. Someone broke into me and my boyfriend's house. Of course we don't live together, but they don't know that. I had to run the story down to them the exact same way I did with the 911 operator.

I sat on the couch, and Vice sat beside me rubbing my arm. He played the concerned boyfriend perfectly, although he was pissed. You wouldn't be able to tell. He gave me kisses on the cheek and held me closely like everything was normal. But I knew he wanted nothing more than to do things his way. In my opinion, that's just stupid. Why would he cover up a crime that really didn't need covering up? A nigga broke in your house, and your girlfriend who happens to have a CCW, killed him. Yeah, it was done with an unregistered gun. But so what? I might get in trouble. At least the gun is clean and the only fingerprints on it is mine. Besides, I don't even think a gun registration is required here in Michigan.

"The man had his gun pointed at your boyfriend and you shot him? Is that correct," asked the cop who's badge read Watkins.

I nodded and wiped tears from my eyes, "I didn't have a choice."

"Thank you officer Watkins, we can take over from here."

I looked past him and into the face of a female detective.

"This bitch," mumbled Vice.

I looked over to him and seen the stress written all over his face. Could this be one of the reasons why he just wanted to get rid of the body? I had no idea he had some shit going on with the police. Of course he does. What the fuck was I thinking?

The lady walked over with a sly smile on her face. Vice on the other hand, wore a mean mug. The meanest mug I've ever seen on him. I felt his heart beating rapidly

US AGAINST EVERYBODY: A DETROIT LOVE TALE 2

against my arm as he pulled me closer and held me tighter. He was furious.

"Good afternoon, Vice," said the detective, totally disregarding me.

But I stepped up. I extended my hand to her and said, "Hi, I'm Storm. I reported the incident."

She glanced at me and lazily gave my hand a shake, "Yes, I'm aware of that. But how about we cut the bull. We all know who pulled the trigger. A felon with no CCW."

Was I supposed to bitch up? Or confess perhaps? Tuh! No honey. I stood my ground. This uptight bitch had me twisted. I was in no shape or form a coward. Obviously I didn't do it but did I tell her that? Did I give her any reason to believe I didn't? Hell no I didn't. When Vice looked at me like I was about to run my mouth, I wiped that look right off of his fine ass face.

I cleared my throat and squinted my eyes to get a better look at her badge, "Um, Detective Olivia Thompson. You must've gotten some false information. I'm no felon, and yes, I do have a CCW. Now if you're referring to Vice as the one who pulled the trigger, than you're wrong. I pulled the trigger. The man was about to blow Vice's head off. I had no choice. There's no telling what he would've done to me next. I'm willing and ready to face the consequences, should there be any."

Detective Olivia didn't turn my way as she spoke directly to Vice, "Is this the type of man you are? A coward who'll let his naïve girlfriend take the murder rap?"

She was trying to get him to fold. I knew how much this was bothering Vice so I prayed like heck he wouldn't confess. I moved my body closer to him, and looked him in the eyes. I searched his hazels for answers but they gave me nothing. Vice was unreadable. I needed him to feel my energy which screamed out 'DON'T CONFESS'.

He shifted in his seat, "Look, finish this shit up aight?"

Vice stood up and walked away after kissing me on the forehead. It pained me to see him walk away defeated. I felt horrible. I should've let him do things his way. I cursed myself for not doing so. Especially when they put the cuffs on me. When they escorted me out of the house, I saw just how much it hurt him. I started to mouth an 'I love you' but he turned away.

*

US AGAINST EVERYBODY: A DETROIT LOVE TALE 2

My palms sweated as I sat there in the interrogation room waiting impatiently to be released. Detective Olivia and her partner continued to question me. They wanted me to fold so badly. But I didn't. I said nothing. I kept directing them to the statement I made at the house. My story would never change. I could never tell on Vice. Snitching just ain't in my blood. Plus, I'd lose it without him. He's become a huge part of my life. Not to have him in it just didn't sit right.

As I sat there, half listening to them my mind was on Mack. So much shit was going on! I couldn't wrap my head around one thing before something else was thrown my way. He was constantly blowing my phone up. My mother was respecting my 'I need space' wishes though. Mack needed to hear my voice. He wanted my forgiveness and that's just not something he was going to get from me. My heart was literally broken. Our relationship will never be the same.

The lengths he went to keep me from a man who's done nothing but make me happy. Sure he lives a crazy life, but peep… it's a crazy life I'm willing to live with him. I didn't realize how accepting I've become until the Joslyn incident. He looked out for me. Regardless of the history he shared with that girl, he was willing to put a bullet in her head. All for disrespecting me. I was precious to him, and because of that, he'll always be precious to me. That's just the way things are.

٭ What's crazy is the fact that we've only been seeing each other for about six months. And in those six months I've been through shit I've never thought I would. I wouldn't change one bit about it though. What we've been through is a token of our love.

"Storm, don't you say another word," said the sharply dressed man carrying a briefcase who entered the room. I didn't know who the hell he was

Detective Olivia was busy leaning over the table in my face. Obviously I wasn't paying her any attention. You see what my mind was on. It was like she wasn't even standing in front of me.

"I haven't," I hesitated to respond.

"Great," he turned to the detectives, "Is my client charged with anything? There was an invasion of her property. Therefore she killed the victim out of self-defense. And as far as the unregistered handgun goes, we all know registration isn't a requirement here in Michigan. My client is free to go."

I stood up and the stepped aside. His client? I don't have a lawyer.

"This isn't the end, Storm. I will be to see you."

US AGAINST EVERYBODY: A DETROIT LOVE TALE 2

"And if need be, my client will press harassment charges against you Detective Thompson," said the attorney with his hand on the small of my back leading me out of the room.

When we were out of the police station I asked who he was and who sent him. He told me his name was Carlyle and he was sent by Vice.

I shook his hand and thanked him. Just as I was about to ask if I could use his phone, Vice's Audi pulled into the parking lot. Carlyle smiled and told me to stay out of trouble before walking away.

Vice got out of the car and opened the passenger door for me. My man looked so stressed despite the forced on smile he wore on his face. I smiled as I walked over to him. He opened his arms for a hug and I did just that. He whispered another apology in my ear and I told him to stop apologizing because I understood completely.

When we let go of one another, his eyes were fixated on the police station. I looked over my shoulder at Detective Thompson who stood at the door with her arms crossed gawking at us. She was going to be a serious problem.

175

"I'm going to have to make that bitch disappear," mumbled Vice as he strapped my seatbelt on after I sat down.

I nodded, "Probably."

He paused before inching himself out of the car. Vice looked me in the eyes and told me he loved me. I kissed him on the lips and told him I loved him too.

*

A month had passed since that crazy shit happened. I still dreamt about how Tank's head split open when Vice shot him in it. Although it was disturbing, what happened doesn't bother me. After we left the police station, we went back to Vice's crib. I took a shower and we left to go view a few properties. There was no way in hell I was going to be staying over there, sleeping in that room after what happened. Since it made me uncomfortable, Vice called his real estate agent before we even went into the house. We weren't living together but he respected me enough to move since I was going to be spending so much time with him.

Speaking of living together, I was giving more thought to that possibility. I was beginning to think it was foolish of us to keep visiting each other when we could simply just stay together under one roof. Anyway, he found a nice three bedroom colonial in Rochester Hills,

US AGAINST EVERYBODY: A DETROIT LOVE TALE 2

MI. I was spending more time there then I was at my condo. I'd hate to move out because he paid the rent up. I'll see if I can get a refund after I talk to him about moving in later on.

Right now I'm at home, having drinks with Carla and Jai. Jai is officially drug free, but shit, she's still a damn drunk. I prefer her to be hooked on liq than coke period.

She shook her head before taking a shot of tequila, "I mean, I had no idea y'all. Ryan seems like the type of nigga who grew up in a happy home with both parents. But he said that was furthest from the truth. What he went through at home is what drove him to coke. I swear I would've never thought. Unlike me, he went to rehab."

"Why did he have the coke in the first place," asked Carla with a mouth full of Doritos.

"He said he kept it as a reminder of a life he used to live," Jai shook her head. "I couldn't have done it. That coke would've been snorted as soon as I left rehab."

We all fell out laughing. I grabbed Carla's bag of chips and ate a hand full before she snatched them away.

I was happy. But every time I looked at Jai a sadness washed over me. I didn't tell her Mack was responsible for her getting shot. I wanted to but I knew it was best left unsaid. She was in a happy place and me telling her that would only piss her off.

"He still on that 'friend' shit," I asked after taking a shot.

"Girl, you know it. But it's nothing. I gotta nigga giving me dick on the regular," she smiled. "Plus, ain't no money shortage honey! The cash is pouring in, if you know what the fuck I mean!"

I rolled my eyes. Her ass was back in the strip club. This time at Erotic City, as a bartender though. I couldn't even judge her. She was addicted to the strip club. That's what she wanted to do. Jai loved easy money. All I cared about was the fact that her nose remained coke free.

"Stop acting like you don't love him," said Carla. "You kill me with that shit. You know damn well you want nothing more than to be with Ryan."

Jai pouted, "Yessss. But he's being mean."

"I don't blame him. You ain't ready for a relationship, Jai. When you are, you'll stop the shit you do," I retorted.

She didn't say anything. She just took another shot, and picked her phone up. I looked at Carla and she looked back at me. We knew what that meant. The

US AGAINST EVERYBODY: A DETROIT LOVE
TALE 2

conversation was over. Jai did that shit every time we
brought up her changing.

[TWELVE]

Jai

I wished they'd just leave the shit alone! I can only handle one thing at a time. Damn, I just kicked the coke habit. I need time to kick the strip club. But let's be honest, that's probably a habit I'll never kick. A bitch loved easy money. There was nothing like making my own shit. I didn't have to ask a man for anything. At least I'm not shaking my ass for ones anymore.

Storm and Carla sat there talking. I was focused on that tattoo on my wrist. Damn I'm mad Ryan peeped that shit. Getting it was a stupid decision I made when I was seventeen. I regretted it. Up until now, no other man I messed with noticed it. It would take the one I was getting feelings for to notice it. I rolled my eyes and threw another shot of Don Julio.

ME (8:12PM): Fuck you, Ryan.

RYAN (8:13PM): U must be drunk n in ur feelings.

US AGAINST EVERYBODY: A DETROIT LOVE TALE 2

I hated how well he knew me. Every time I was drunk, I angry texted him. Shit, I'm pissed. I will never admit how much I really wanted to be with him. Him not fucking with me on that level anymore really upset me.

After every motion I went through as he was weening me off of coke he stayed. When I threatened him, with a knife, he stayed. I told him I'd kill him if he didn't give me the rest of the coke he had. He was only giving me small amounts at a time, following Wikipedia's advice. That shit had me heated. I charged at him, cutting his hand but he managed to take the knife from me. I cried long and hard begging him not to leave. He told me he'd never leave me to suffer alone.

And when I finally kicked the habit...when I no longer craved it...I thought things would go back to how they were before. Boy was I in for a rude awakening. Ryan took me home, told me how proud he was, and drove right off before I could even get inside the house.

I never gave up on trying though. I was even there for him when he was depressed about Branden's murder. I went to the funeral and everything with him. I thought he'd realize I really cared. But he didn't. Ryan thought everything I did had motive. He was confident that I was only trying so hard now because he's been receiving offers from major teams in the NFL. Ryan said I only saw him as a meal ticket. Hell yeah I do, but there's much more to him than just that.

"Damn, bitch, you don't hear us talking to you," yelled Storm pulling me out of my thoughts.

Branden's murder briefly coming to mind made me ask her what I've been asking since it happened.

"You still don't know how your dad knew B?"

Storm rolled her eyes, "For the hundredth time, no Jai I don't. Why do you keep asking me that when you know I haven't spoken to Mack in over a month? You know we're not cool."

"I just figured you'd want answers. I'm just saying, I sure would."

"I simply don't give a fuck, sis," She took a shot and then laughed, "Got damn!"

I stared at her. There was something she was keeping from me. The shit didn't sit well with me because we told each other everything. I glanced at Carla to see if I could read her. I wondered if Carla knew what I didn't. Carla seemed just as confused as me. Storm was changing. And I won't say it was a bad change. She was no longer a goody-goody. Fucking with a real nigga will do that to

US AGAINST EVERYBODY: A DETROIT LOVE TALE 2

you. But what I didn't like is the fact that she was obviously hiding something from me.

"Mmhmm, whatever bitch. We gotta talk later," I told her.

She waved me off, "Annnywaaay, as I was saying! We wanna go to Erotic City and make it rain on a few bad bitches. You down?"

I giggled, "Yeah, bitch, of course! I didn't want to see the inside of that club tonight since I'm off, but fuck it. Maybe boss man will let me hop on stage," I joked as I stood up from the couch and walked towards the bathroom.

I was staggering so bad that Storm had to help me walk.

"Oh no, ho! You ain't hoping on no stage, the fuck."

"Keep calm, I was just joking," I told her before almost falling

"Maybe we should stay home. You drunk as fuck Jai."

183

"I'll be good in a few," I said, waving her off.

"If you ain't a little better by 11:30 we ain't going," she told me matter-of-factly.

I looked at her as we walked to the bathroom. Carla was sitting on the couch, on her phone. I needed Storm to tell me what she was hiding. I asked her if she was keeping something from me. She just laughed and said she didn't tell me everything. She thought the shit was a joke but I was dead ass serious.

"I thought we told each other everything, sis."

Storm sighed and helped me get my yoga pants down. See, this is why I love her! She looks out for me like no other. But she was keeping secrets and that's not how we got down.

"We do, Jai. God, please don't kill my vibe," said Storm as I plopped down on the toilet.

I held my head down, "I know you're hiding somethin—

"If it's still bugging you tomorrow, we'll talk then okay?"

I looked up at her and smiled, "I love you, sister."

She frowned up, "I love yo drunk ass too." She laughed and walked out of the bathroom.

US AGAINST EVERYBODY: A DETROIT LOVE TALE 2

[THIRTEEN]
Vice

I was at Erotic City, with Reek and Dawson, getting a lap dance from a bad ass dark skin bitch. The size of her ass was ridiculous! The way her ass cheeks bounced in sync with the beat drove a nigga crazy. I was originally here for business but once that shit was taken care of, the boss man sent the baddest bitches in the club to our section.

I was lifted. Shit was gravy in the hood. I didn't have any fuck niggas out to get me – well not to my knowledge at least. So I was kicking back. I had just blew about three kush blunts back to back, and was getting wasted off of Dusse. Tonight was a good night. Not only was I drama free, but me and the owner just made a sweet deal that I was getting 50k out of easy!

I closed my eyes and enjoyed the feeling of Dark Chocolate grinding on the imprint bulging out of my True Religion jeans. Ay, a nigga was just having fun. Fuck I look like turning down a lap dance? If brown skin was here it'd be a different story. I'd never disrespect her like that. But now, she was at the crib kicking back with her girls. And I'm at the strip club enjoying myself. Ain't like I'm about to stick my dick in thi—

"Ay! Hold up, baby girl," I said as I jumped back and grabbed my jeans. Bitch was unzipping my pants. I didn't even realize she wasn't grinding on me. If I would've been paying attention, I would've known she was on her knees. She was getting ready to dome me up in a club full of people. Not to mention, my niggas were right on side of me.

I turned my head in their directions and both them niggas were getting head. Type of shit is this? I looked out past our section and the boss was holding his glass up nodding at me. I looked down at the broad in between my legs and told her she had to bounce.

"But, I want to," she moaned as she reached out and touched my dick, "And it's so big, daddy."

I put my hand up, blocking her from grabbing me again, "I said get yo tricking ass the fuck from round here."

"I was told to show you a good time so that's what I'm doing."

US AGAINST EVERYBODY: A DETROIT LOVE TALE 2

What was leaving her mouth no longer mattered. What the hell was she doing here?

Storm stood right outside of our section with pain written all over her face. Instead of saying something that would've helped my situation I said, "What you doing here, lil mama?"

Dark Chocolate looked over her shoulder and stood up. She rolled her eyes and sucked her teeth as she made her way to the stage. Storm was unmoving. Lil' mama was pissed. I buttoned my jeans up and walked up to her. She put her hand up and walked away. I spoke to Jai and Carla but neither of them said a word to me.

"Don't be stupid. Both y'all know fuck well it wasn't what it looked like," I said to them before following Storm out of the club.

I maneuvered through the crowd as quickly as possible. Erotic City was slapping!

When I finally made it outside, I looked left and right in search for her. I peeped her speed walking to the parking lot and ran after her. I called her name and she looked over her shoulder and kept walking. Why the fuck

187

was she being so damn childish? Storm knows me and she know I'm not even cut like that. What type of nigga do she think I am?

Finally, I caught up with her just as she was getting in the car. She looked at me out of the window and shifted the car in drive. I rain over to the passenger side and hopped in just as she was pulling off.

"Why you bugging lil' mama? You know I'm not even—

"Get out," said Storm pointing out of the car.

"Stop playing with me, girl."

"Ain't nobody playing in this mothafucka! Gone back in the club nigga! Finish getting yo lil' dick sucked."

I laughed, "Come on now, shorty, you know got damn well a nigga's dick ain't lil."

I was on some play-play shit but she wasn't having it. Storm didn't even crack a smile.

I held my hands up, "Aight, you don't feel like playing. But peep, if you want to know the real, carry yo ass back in the club and ask the bitch what my dick look like."

Storm pressed down on the brakes and frowned up, "Nigga, are you serious? Vice get out!"

US AGAINST EVERYBODY: A DETROIT LOVE
TALE 2

I stared at her for a minute, and then nodded my head, "Aight cool, you still wanna be on some mad shit huh? Storm, pull off."

"What? No! I said—

"I said pull over," I yelled, causing her to flinch.

She briefly stared at me before speeding off, "You're going home."

I didn't say anything to her. I just let her ride, while staring at her. She was furious. But for what though? Her goofy ass knows damn well I wasn't getting my dick sucked. She's acting out. Lil' mama ain't herself when she's been lackin'.

I rubbed on the inside of her thigh. Just as I expected, she moaned and closed her eyes.

"You're driving," I told her.

Storm opened her eyes and glanced at me, "Stop."

Her mouth was telling me to stop, but her body was responding in a way that told me she wanted the exact opposite. I eased my hand up her thigh and rubbed on her

189

pussy through the thin fabric of her leggings. She closed her eyes again. I leaned over and whispered in her ear, "Open your eyes, Storm."

Her eyes fluttered open and a moan escaped her mouth. She glanced at me again. Her eyes were full of passion. But again, the word stop spilled from her lips.

"You don't want me to stop, brown skin. Keep it G with a nigga," I said as I whispered in her ear before kissing her neck.

"You're going to…going to make me crash."

I rubbed her clit in a circular motion, "No I'm not. Just keep—

"Oh God…please… Stop Vice."

"Stop doing that, Storm."

She stopped at a red light and turned towards me. I peeped how she slightly opened her legs further, "Stop doing what?"

"Begging me to stop, when stopping is the last thing you want me to do."

I grabbed the back of her neck with my freehand and pulled her into a kiss. The kiss held so much passion that we didn't realize when the light turned green. The cars behind us honked their horns and I pulled away so that she could pull off.

US AGAINST EVERYBODY: A DETROIT LOVE TALE 2

"Where are we going," asked Storm as she panted heavily.

I pulled away from the kiss, that didn't mean I stopped playing with that phat pussy though.

"Pull over."

Her eyes damn near popped out of her head, "What?!"

I leaned over again, and whispered in her ear as I felt the fabric of her leggings getting damp.

"You really wanna ride all the way to the crib," I unbuckled my jeans and pulled my dick out, "Come on now, brown skin. You know you can't wait just as much as I can't."

She glanced at my dick and pulled over into an abandoned parking lot.

Storm shut the engine off and nervously looked around, "What if someone sees us, Vice?"

I unzipped her North Face hoodie and caressed her nipples through her T-shirt, "the windows are tinted. If

191

they weren't, do you think I'd even let shit pop off out here?" My hand slowly eased up her shirt, "Relax, baby."

She seductively looked at me, bit her bottom lip, and then leaned over and wrapped her full lips around my dick. I threw my head back on the headrest while she skillfully moved her mouth up and down on my dick. Storm was good at many, many things but what stood out the most was her head game.

Most people don't like eye contact during oral sex, but I love the shit. Especially the way she's looking at me now. My dick was glistening with spit; Storm made sure my dick was always heavily coated with her saliva. She cupped my balls as she slowly eased my dick down her throat. Her gag reflex was nonexistent. Storm grabbed my hand and placed it on the back of her head. She loved that rough shit, so I gave it to her.

"Fuck my face," said Storm.

I slid the seat back further and she climbed in between my legs. I kicked my pants to my ankles and I bit my bottom lip as I did what I was told. I grabbed a fist full of her expensive ass weave and slammed my dick in and out of her mouth. With my other hand I reached down and pinched her nipples. She moaned on my dick, and then removed it from her mouth. Storm looked up at me as she slapped it on her face, on some porno type shit.

My eyes rolled into the back of my head when she put her mouth on both of my balls, and stroked me

US AGAINST EVERYBODY: A DETROIT LOVE TALE 2

simultaneously. I grabbed the sides of her face and moved her from dick. I couldn't take it anymore. My mouth salivated at the thought of her on my tongue.

I took her leggings completely off. I stared at the beautifulness of her pussy before lifting her off her feet. I placed her legs on side of my face, which was nestled in between her legs. She held the back of my head from leverage.

"I'm going to fall," said Storm going into a fit of giggles.

"I got you, baby. You ain't going nowhere, girl," I told her as I buried my face in her pussy.

She moaned and grinded on my face. Shit, a nigga liked to have his face fucked too. I loved when she did that wild shit. I pulled her closer to me, as I licked the slit in her pussy, spreading her lips. I wrapped one arm around her back, and with the other I reached up. I twisted her nipple in between my index finger and thumb.

She moaned and then yelled, "Vice don't...don't drop me."

193

But I did. I dropped her right on top of my dick. I was tripping because I didn't even have on a rubber. We were in the moment. I was in the moment. Only pussy I'm sliding in his hers. Only dick hitting her sweet pussy walls is me. She didn't seem to mind. Nah, not one bit.

A nigga almost came while staring in her eyes. So fucking sexy. Pussy so damn tight. So fucking good. Damn. I gripped her waist as she slowly grinded on me. Her mouth was slightly ajar, so I covered it with mine. Storm slid her tongue in my mouth and I softly sucked on it.

"Mmh, I taste sweet," said Storm while licking her lips.

A fucking freak. I loved it. Her saying that sent me over the edge. It was like she had awakened a monster inside of me. I turned her around, so that she would be riding reverse cowgirl. I ran my hands down her back. Lil mama so official, even her back is sexy. I leaned up a little and made a trail of kisses from the back of her neck to the middle of her back. She was loving it. The way she softly moaned my name drove me crazy.

I grabbed her waist and made circles in her pussy with my dick. She told me I was hitting her spot, so I kept at it. I chewed on my bottom lip in awe. My dick was covered in white cream. She was so fucking wet, I had to stop myself from cumming. I lifted her off my dick, and slammed her back on it.

US AGAINST EVERYBODY: A DETROIT LOVE TALE 2

"Ahhh, wait...shit...fuck," yelled Storm as she bucked on me.

I smacked her ass and told her to take this dick. She looked at me over her shoulder and for a second there, I got lost in her seductive eyes. Had a nigga about to switch up on some love making shit. So I tore my eyes away from hers and left them fixated on the dimples in her lower back.

I gripped her ass cheeks, spreading them apart so I could dig deeper. Her pussy made a gushy noise. She clinched her pussy muscles on me and told me she was about to cum. I lifted her, removing my dick from her pussy and placed it in between her ass cheeks. She moved her body in the same motion as she was when she rode me. There was white cream all over the crack of her ass. For what seemed like the hundredth time, my mouth salivated.

"Put yo hands on the dash, Storm."

She did, and looked back at me. I moved my body back, and my face forward. I've never been an ass eating type of nigga but there was something irresistible about the way her ass looked covered in her own juices.

195

Spreading her ass cheeks open, I slid my tongue down her crack.

"Damn," I said as I brought her closer to me.

She looked over her shoulder and down at me as I lapped my tongue all over her.

"Please….fuck me Vice."

I stopped and looked up at her, "You know I love when you beg for—

Before I could finish my shit talking, she was on me. This time, straddling me with her arms draped over my shoulders. She looked into my eyes with brown eyes flooded with passion.

"So fucking sexy," said Storm before kissing me.

She bounced on me, giving me more pleasure than I had ever experienced. The pussy hugged me like it was made specifically for my dick. I felt an orgasm coming but I didn't stop. I kept going. Telling myself I would pull out before it was too late.

Storm placed her feet on side of me and bent her knees. I had full access to the pussy.

"Oh my God! So fucking…fucking big," she yelled as she slowed her pace.

I grabbed her hips and increased her rhythm, "Uhhh…pussy too good lil' mama."

US AGAINST EVERYBODY: A DETROIT LOVE TALE 2

Her eyes, that were once closed, shot open, "Don't...don't cum inside...inside of me Vice."

"Shhhh," I told her before covering my mouth with hers.

She tried to get off of me, but I firmly held onto her. Her pussy had a hold on me. I knew I was fucking up, but that didn't stop me from busting inside of her.

After we finished, she didn't get up like I expected her too. Instead, she laid her head on my chest with her arms wrapped around my neck. I reclined the seat, and wrapped my arms around her petite body. We both were in our thoughts. Me, I was thinking about how good the pussy just was. I knew what she was thinking about. And it wasn't about how good the fucking was neither. She was bugging because I came inside of her. Worried. I knew this because of the look in her eyes when I looked down at her.

"Why you trippin, lil' mama?"

She looked up at me, "I don't want to get pregnant, Vice."

"You won't. You poppin' them pills now right?"

She was quiet for a minute and I asked her again.

"No..."

I laughed, "But brown skin, you told me you were going to get them after the last slip up."

This was my second time busting a nut in shorty. She told me she was going to get some birth control. I'm not tripping on nothing. I'm just wondering why she didn't get them when she said she would. Anybody as pissed as she was, would've ran to the doctor.

"I forgot."

I twisted my lips at her, "Yeah, aight lil mama. You forgot."

She playfully punched me in the chest, "I'm serious, big head. I did forget."

I smirked at her and she punched me again. Storm got off my lap and touched the door handle like she was about to get out of the car with nothing covering her ass.

"Fuck you doing?"

She looked at me over her shoulder, "I have to get something out of the trunk."

I picked her up and sat her in the driver's seat. I pulled my bottoms up and said, "Fuck you thinking

US AGAINST EVERYBODY: A DETROIT LOVE
TALE 2

about? Tryna go outside with yo ass exposed. I'll grab it,
open the trunk."

She laughed, hit the trunk button.

As soon as I stepped out the car, a chill came over
me. It's cold out, but this was a different type of chill.
The same feeling I got on the block, when niggas came
through blasting. I looked over my shoulder, and to my
left and right. Nothing was out of the ordinary. I
proceeded to walk to the back of the car.

Storm lowered her window and told me to grab her
Nike gym bag. I opened the trunk, the feeling came
again. I looked around. Nothing but stillness. It was pitch
black out, with the exception of a street light that
occasionally flickered off and on. My heart rate sped up
and I cursed myself. I was out here naked. I had no plans
on leaving the club with Storm. I didn't even know shorty
was coming through. This was spontaneous. I hated
spontaneity.

I didn't have my burner and that shit bothered me.
Had I been thinking straight and not on no emotional shit,
I would've stopped at my car and grabbed it. The gun

199

wasn't allowed in the club. That bitch sat comfortably under my driver's seat.

"Hop on the passenger side," I told her in a voice barely above a whisper.

I didn't know what the fuck was going on and I'd be damned if I get caught out here with my girl. I wanted to keep her away from this shit. Something was going on and I needed to get the fuck out of dodge before we were ambushed.

"Why," yelled Storm.

I sighed. I slowly walked to the driver's side of the car, carefully watching my surroundings. As I stared at her, I saw a light flicker from the corner of my eyes.

"Move over, Storm."

"No, I want to dr—

I tossed the bag over my shoulder, then yanked the door open. I lifted her from the seat and sat her on the passenger side. Somebody was out here. Like I said, I didn't have my burner and if these niggas came at us I'd be at a disadvantage. I didn't want to be at a disadvantage; definitely not with wifey with me.

I joked around with her so much that she didn't realize I was serious. I needed her to take this shit serious I didn't want to be a rude nigga. I tried my best not to but what she did next, annoyed me.

US AGAINST EVERYBODY: A DETROIT LOVE TALE 2

She sucked her teeth, reached over, cut the car off, and snatched the key out. I glared at her as I snatched the key out of her hand and quickly started it back up. I jerked the car in drive and sped off. I kept my eye on the rearview mirror and noticed a black van pull from behind the abandoned store.

"Fuck," I yelled.

"What's wrong with you? Why you acting so funky," asked Storm as she rummaged through her gym bag, oblivious to how real shit was about to get.

"Something's not right," I punched the steering wheel, "And I'm fucking naked out here."

"Calm down," she said as she cleaned her pussy with a Wet Wipe.

"What the fuck you mean calm down, brown skin? Shit's about to pop off and..." I paused, "What are you doing?"

She gave me a look as to say 'duh', "I'm cleaning myself, Vice." She tossed the Wet Wipe in the trashcan on the floor and then slid on a pair of lace boy shorts. "Calm down though, alright? We good."

Despite me driving, I closed my eyes and ran my hands down my face. She was too naïve to realize what the fuck was popping off.

"I need to get you home right now," I punched the steering wheel again, "Shit, I don't need you out here caught up in this shit. Especially not while I'm naked."

I glanced at her and she was shaking her head. Storm opened her glove compartment and retrieved the Pink 9mm I made sure she copped a couple weeks ago. She handed it to me and said, "You might be naked, but I'm not." She winked, "I got you baby."

I took the gun from her and smirked, "Shorty…you's a mothafuckin rider." I looked in the rearview and noticed the van a few feet behind us, "I still need you to get home."

"I'm not leaving you," she yelled.

"Storm, stop fucking with me aight?"

"We're in this to—

"I'm in this alone! I don't want you involved in this lifestyle," I yelled, cutting her off. "Listen baby, I'm not being me—

"Rather you like it or not, I'm involved with you meaning I'm involved with it. Deal with it. Accept it,

US AGAINST EVERYBODY: A DETROIT LOVE
TALE 2

because I had to." She told me with her arms crossed over
her chest.

I didn't give a fuck about what she was rapping
about. I had to figure out how I was going to make this
work without getting her hurt in the process. I turned into
the parking lot of Erotic City and the van kept driving.

I let out a sigh of relief and pulled up next to my
whip. I shifted her car in park and told her to go home
right now. She told me she had to get Jai and Carla. I shut
the engine off and walked inside the club with her to get
her girls.

As soon as they left, me and my niggas did too.

*

Hours had passed by and I was still out, circling
blocks trying to find that black van. The digital numbers
on my phone read *5:12AM*. I had just ignored yet another
call from Wifey. She wanted me home. But being at
home was the last thing on my mind. I was focused on
finding them fuck niggas before they found me. I didn't

even know who they were. Shit, it could've been anybody.

I still didn't know who was behind that drive by on the block a couple months ago. It could've been Mack but the more I think about it, it could've been Tank and them too. Too many questions were unanswered for me to just go home and try to sleep. I wouldn't be able to anyway. My mind would constantly be on that black van, and what possessed them to try to ride down on me. Didn't niggas know by now that I wasn't to be fucked with? I had made an example out of a few niggas in the last couple months. That should've been a warning. All that bloodshed probably did was cause more animosity in niggas hearts. Pissed a few fuck niggas off. Made them want to go against death, when that shit ain't even possible.

I turned on Brentwood and said, "I'm probably in the wrong mothafuckin hood. Let me swing over on the six."

"Man, let's finish this shit tomorrow. You ain't about to find no black van out here at five in the morning, bro," said Reek with the passenger seat reclined, half sleep.

I glanced at him but said nothing, as I made my way back on Van Dyke. He wanted to sleep. And I wanted to spill blood. I gripped my heat as I drove with one hand. I glanced at Dawson in the backseat and caught him shaking his head. These niggas didn't want to ride with me, so they didn't have to.

US AGAINST EVERYBODY: A DETROIT LOVE
TALE 2

I jerked the car in park and said, "Get out."

Reek lifted up and said, "Aw shit, this nigga
bugging."

"Not bugging my nigga. Just sick and tired of you
pussy niggas complaining." I stared outside through my
rearview mirror with my finger on the trigger, waiting for
something to pop off. I turned my attention back to Reek
and said, "Aint no point of you females riding with me if
y'all ain't ready for something to pop off!"

"That's the thing cuz, ain't shit about to pop off. You
being 'noid as usual," said Dawson.

I laughed, "Ayo, I said get the fuck out."

Reek shook his head full of dreads and said, "I'm
riding with you bro. stop bugging."

I yelled, "I said get the fuck out! I don't need no
pussy niggas riding with me. Apparently I'm the only
nigga ready for war! Y'all on some soft, sucka shit and I
don't need that negative energy around me."

Reek unhooked his seatbelt and said, "Aight man," he looked over his shoulder at Dawson and said, "Ay cuz, you can crash at my spot since I'm just a few blocks up."

Dawson nodded and opened the door.

"Glad you fuck niggas could sort shit out," I said before I sped off after they hopped out.

I didn't know where I was headed but I knew what I was looking for. A black conversion van missing a hubcap. I rubbed my eyes as I drove down six mile, heading west. I didn't even have beef with niggas over there but that was just to my knowledge. Them fuck boys could've came from anywhere. I figured I'd search the hoods I'm constantly in first.

My phone rang again and I stared at her pretty brown face. I need to answer it. Lil' mama's probably over there worried as fuck. I haven't talked to her since Erotic City. I couldn't. Brown skin was a distraction I didn't need right now. I stopped at a red light on six mile and Vandyke, just as I was about to ignore her call. Instead, I choose to answer it.

"Skin tone like Hershey's, body lord have mercy," I said reciting lyrics from Fabolous's Ready.

"Vicccce stop kidding. Where are you," asked Storm, her voice sounding groggy.

"I'll be there in a bit, baby, go to sleep."

US AGAINST EVERYBODY: A DETROIT LOVE TALE 2

"Come home now. It's late. Nothing is going on…"

As she spoke, my attention was fixated elsewhere. There was an altercation going on at the Marathon gas station across from where I was. I wouldn't have gave a fuck had it been two niggas scrapping but there was a man beating the fuck out of a woman. I wanted to mind my own damn business but you already know how I feel about fuck shit going on in my presence.

"I'll be there soon," I said to Storm while she was talking. I hung up before she even replied.

I threw my phone on the seat, beside my gun, and turned into the gas station. I stopped inches from them. By then, the girl was lying on the ground. I hopped out the whip just as my mans was bringing his foot down on the poor girl's face.

He glanced over at me, "Mind your own business man."

I didn't say anything to him. Instead, I walked up to him and gave him a quick two-piece, knocking him out cold. He fell back onto the concrete, with a loud thud.

Blood leaked from his head instantly. I tore my eyes away from him and onto the girl.

I extended my hand to her, to help her up. When she looked up at me with familiar light brown eyes, I gasped out of surprise.

Laila?

US AGAINST EVERYBODY: A DETROIT LOVE
TALE 2

[FOURTEEN]

Storm

I woke up alone. That'd be all fine and dandy if I was at home. But I wasn't. I was at Vice's house waiting on him. Last night he was busy doing whatever the hell he does when he's avoiding me. I knew he was out taking care of business but a part of me felt that he was cheating. He wouldn't do that right? Vice cared for me, deeply. Hell, Nico claimed to care about me too but that didn't stop him from sticking his dick in any thick bitch that came his way.

I grabbed my phone from the nightstand and couldn't believe it was almost noon. Where in the fuck is he? See, this is the type of shit I will not put up with. I did enough of waking up alone, and crying with Nico. Fuck that. And to top everything off, he hadn't even called or texted me.

209

I sat up and called him. Just as I expected, he didn't pick up. Out of frustration, I threw my phone across the room. I should've been worried about his well-being but instead, I was on some insecure shit. Can you blame me? I've been hurt too many times before and Vice is a fine ass nigga that's wanted by numerous bitches. But will my man do that? He's a man, of course he will! I was bugging... answering my own questions. I just needed to know where he was.

I paced the floor, biting on my nails, trying to think of what to do. I couldn't do anything. I didn't know how to get in touch with anybody that knew him. I could go over to the spot but he didn't want me over there. Times are desperate though. Fuck what he want and don't want.

I carried my naked ass to the bathroom. Yes, bitch, I was butt booty naked waiting on him to come home. I was waiting and ready to start part two of last night. That shit gave me an adrenaline rush. Quiet as kept, I peeped the black van before him. I didn't see who was on the inside but I saw it. Keep calm, I wasn't being reckless. I was getting my kicks off. I rode his dick reverse cowgirl, eyes on the van, wondering if they could see the fuck faces I made. Not because I wanted them to, but because the thought of someone being able to see what that dick did to me, turned me on. I felt foolish afterwards. I know, I should've said something but I didn't think much of it. Not until he was freaking out about it.

US AGAINST EVERYBODY: A DETROIT LOVE TALE 2

I started the shower and got inside. What if whoever it was had him? My heart rate sped up and I cursed myself. Fuck! I should've told him I peeped them last night. Maybe he could've ran up on the van and murked them off. I shook my head. Look at the way I'm speaking. Fucking with Vice was definitely changing me. I wasn't sure if that was a good thing or a bad thing? For now, let's call it a good thing. Dealing with a man like him, you have to possess some type of gangsta!

I got in the shower. As the water cascaded over my body, my hands found my stomach. What if I'm pregnant? I can't be! This nigga lives a life too damn crazy. I do too, since I'm a part of it. A child is the last thing we need. I made a mental note to grab a morning after pill before I did anything else.

*

An hour later I dressed casually in a pair of stonewash jeggings, a red crew neck sweater that read 'CELFIE', and some red, black, and white Huaraches. I had my Mink Brazilian hair bone straight. Before heading out, I grabbed my designer bag, phone, and keys off the kitchen island.

My phone rung, *Carla.*

I answered, "Hey, girl."

"Storm…don't trip."

"What bitch," I asked with an attitude as I locked the house up.

"I just seen Vice at The Westin in Southfield," said Carla hesitantly.

I sighed out of relief, "God! You found him!" I paused, "What the fuck you doing at The Westin? Ain't you supposed to be at work?"

"I ended up calling off. I met Pierre there last night," she hurried her words as she spoke, "That's beside the point! Vice was walking with a bitch."

I stopped dead in my tracks. I was on my way to my car but when those words left her lips, I was stuck in the driveway.

"Say what?"

"Storm, don—

I hung up and jetted to my car. I had to get there before his sneaky, cheating ass left. I couldn't believe he was doing me like this. Thing is, I was so fucking upset

US AGAINST EVERYBODY: A DETROIT LOVE
TALE 2

that I couldn't even cry. Nah, instead of sadness I was full of anger. How he rapping all that he ain't trying to lose me shit in my ear when he really don't give a damn? I took a murder rap for him! I could've went to fucking jail! I went against my family for him! And this is how he thanks me!?

I started my car and sped away from the house, in the direction of the freeway. The speed limit was only fifty, but I did seventy there. I prayed to God hook didn't catch up with me. They stayed on that bull shit in Rochester. The last thing I needed was to be pulled over before getting a chance to cut the niggas dick clean off. Yes, it's just that serious. Thing is though, the only thing I have on me is this burner. Fuck it, I'm shooting it off.

I kept my eyes on the rearview as I hopped on the freeway. As badly as I tried to stop from crying, I couldn't help it. They weren't sad tears, believe that! They were mad tears. He was just like Nico. I told him how much that weak ass nigga hurt me. And you know what he said? Ran that same ass game. *See, naw, brown skin you're too much of a fuckin' diamond to even think about cheating on. That nigga was a clown. Glad he fucked up though, otherwise I would've missed out on this blessing.* I can't believe I fell for that shit. I could clearly see how though. He spoke with so much passion, like he really meant what he said. Like I was literally a diamond and not a fucking human being. I believed him because he spoke from his soul.

The game he ran was unlike anything I've ever experienced. Every time I said he was running game, he'd look me straight in the eyes... you know, with them sexy colored ones with the hazel hue. And he'd tell me he wasn't running game. Said he was speaking from the heart. Tuh! Speaking from his dick! All niggas gave a damn about was taking care of their dicks. They couldn't give a fuck less about taking care of a woman's heart. I thought Vice was different. I thought wrong.

Twenty minutes later I was making a right on Central Park Boulevard. I was full of so much rage, that my hands were trembling. Hell, my entire body was trembling. With my shaky left hand, I wiped tears from my eyes. I turned into the parking lot, searching for a spot.

Maybe Carla didn't see Vice. Maybe it was just someone who looked like him. I bet that's it. Watch when I walk up to that desk and give them his name. They won't know what the hell I'm talking about that. I was in denial. But my denial was put to hush once I laid eyes on his car. It could've been anyone's Audi right? Not with the same fucking license plate number. Yes, I know it all. That was all the confirmation I needed.

US AGAINST EVERYBODY: A DETROIT LOVE TALE 2

I hurried up and found me a parking spot. My heart thumped rapidly. I was full of anticipation. I told myself what I was going to do when I saw him, but there's no telling what the hell I'm going to do. Seeing it and imagining seeing it are two totally different things. I couldn't deal. I can't even stomach thinking of him with another female. To find out he spent the night with someone else last night was killing me. That's why he was on some flaky, weird shit when we spoke.

I opened my glove box, eying the pink handgun. Did I really need that shit? I'm not a fucking killer, but I want to kill his ass. The thoughts I was having told me I loved him more than I realized. We've only been together for about seven months but man…I love him more than I've ever loved a man.

I shook my head and slammed the glove box. I don't need to catch a body for real this time. I'd definitely spend some time in jail. That would be premediated like a mothafucka. I got out of the car empty handed. I didn't even carry my bag with me. I didn't need anything in my hands. These hitters had to be free, in case I had to beat the fuck out of somebody up there.

After being given information, I headed to his suite. Vice went all out. They were staying in the Luxury Suite. She must be something special. I felt a lump in my throat and told myself it wasn't time to be shedding some pussy ass tears! I shook it off and held my head up as I treaded to his room.

Finally, I stood outside of the door. I took a deep breath, and knocked.

A few seconds later, he answered. Vice looked like he saw a fucking ghost. I wiped that surprise right off of his face. Yup, switched it right to anger after I punched him in the jaw.

Immediately, he grabbed me by my wrist and pulled me into his chest.

"Ay, what the fuck is wrong with you girl? What are you even doing here," yelled Vice so close to my face I could smell the Colgate toothpaste on his breath.

"No, Vice what the fuck you doing here? Where the bitch at, huh!? Where she at," I yelled as I struggled to escape his embrace. But it was useless.

Vice had a grip on me so tight, I struggled to breathe. He was furious. I hit him hard as hell, I didn't hold back. So I could understand his anger but I didn't give a fuck about it.

"Vice…is everything okay,"

US AGAINST EVERYBODY: A DETROIT LOVE TALE 2

My eyes darted in the direction of the voice and I went crazy. There was a fucking woman in here! I tried my damnedest to get away. At this point, Vice had lifted me from my feet. He tossed me over my shoulder, but that grip didn't loosen up. I was pissed.

"Let me go! Let me go," I yelled and screamed like a mad woman. "Had me up waiting and worried about you and you're out fucking with some...some basic bitch!"

She was basic. Basic and badly beaten. Her light skin had bruises all over it. Although the crisp white tank she wore covered her upper body, I could tell there were bruises on her chest. They were all over her. The ones on her neck were the most vivid. Her curly, sandy brown hair was disheveled. Her light brown eyes had black rings around them. There was a split down her full bottom lip. The more I looked at her, the more her beauty shone through her wounds. Immediately, I felt self-conscious. She was beautiful under the bruises. Realizing how pretty she actually was, made my stomach drop. And there was a certain pain in my heart that I couldn't really describe. You know, the pain of a broken heart.

"Storm! Calm the fuck down! Or I swear to God," yelled Vice.

"Or what nigga, or what?!" I asked as I beat him in the head.

He tried to dodge my hits without releasing his grip. But he couldn't. He let me go and I fell on the floor. He looked over his shoulder, down at me on the floor with sadness in his eyes.

"Shit, brown skin, you alright?"

I was embarrassed. The woman stood over by the window with her head down. She looked over at us every now and then.

I kicked at him, "Leave me alone, Vice…" The tears I tried so hard to fight back, spilled out of my eyes with a vengeance. Like they were mad at me for fighting them so long. I boohooed like never before. "I can't…I can't believe you're doing this…this to me." I was crying so hard I could barely talk or breath.

Vice kneeled down next to me. He reached out for me despite the hits I was throwing at him. He didn't even bother shielding himself. After fighting him for so long, I gave up. I let him grab me. He held me so tight. This time instead of anger, I felt love oozing from his pores.

He buried his face in my neck as always, and inhaled.

US AGAINST EVERYBODY: A DETROIT LOVE TALE 2

Vice whispered in my ear, "Shhh. You doing all of this shit for nothing, brown skin." He kissed me on the cheek. As bad as I wanted to jerk away, I didn't. His lips felt so good on my skin. I cursed myself for loving him so much.

"She's my sister," said Vice.

I pulled away from him and looked into his hazel brown eyes. The ones that always look so dreamy. So fucking seductive. The sexiness of him so was effortless.

"What? You think I believe that—

"Think back, lil' mama."

I was silent as I thought back. On our first date, he mentioned a sister he hadn't seen since he was a child. I covered my mouth out of shock, and looked over at her. She was sitting on the couch, with her head hanging low.

"Seriou...seriously?"

He nodded, "Her name is Laila."

Vice stood up, and extended his hand to help me to my feet.

"Where did you…how did you find her," I asked. I was in so much shock I could barely speak.

"We'll talk about that later."

Vice held onto my hand and we walked over to the couch where she was sitting. She looked so worn out, and sad. Whoever beat her ass, did a number on her.

"I truly apologize. I didn't know," I told her. I was even more embarrassed than before.

She looked up at with a half-smile, "It's okay. I'm Laila. You…you must be Storm."

"Yes, I'm Storm. Trust me, I'm not usually this crazy."

"Fuck out of here lying lil' mama. You crazy," yelled Vice from the back of the room. I didn't even notice him walking off.

I told her to ignore him. I sat next to her and noticed how timid she was. She was more embarrassed than me. I couldn't believe he found his sister. I'm sure they had a lot to catch up on, so I understood why he didn't answer or call me. Not to mention, her face is fucked up. Somebody used her ass as a punching bag. Vice hated everything about domestic violence. I know by what he did to Joslyn that's hard to believe. But he didn't hit her. He just scared her… almost killed the bitch.

US AGAINST EVERYBODY: A DETROIT LOVE TALE 2

"You okay," I asked. I knew that was a stupid ass question but what else am I supposed to say?

"Trying to be," she nervously laughed. "I know I look a mess. Talk about first impressions."

I laughed, "Exactly. I was acting a complete fool."

"I understand completely," she nodded and said. "You seem like a sweet girl, despite trying to attack me a minute ago."

We shared a laugh. I was glad the awkwardness was over. Although she still seemed nervous, we casually conversed. I learned a lot about her in such a short period of time. She told me Vice saved her. I giggled and told her he kind of did the same thing for me. If it wasn't for Vice, that guy probably would've seriously put hands on me. Vice is such a fucking boss its ridiculous.

Anyway, I also learned that she was older than Vice by two years. When I asked her where she been all this time, she tensed up and became silent. So I changed the subject. I figured I was getting too personal, too soon. I decided to keep it at the regular stuff. For a few minutes, I just told her about myself. I didn't want her to think I was prying. I was excited to be getting to know someone in his family besides Dawson. And to be sitting, kicking it with his sister whom he hadn't seen in over fifteen years was big.

Twenty minutes passed before Vice came from the back of the room. Laila excused herself, saying she needed to take a nap. Before she walked off she gave me a hug and slyly winked at Vice. Her ass didn't need a nap. She was simply trying to give us some privacy.

As soon as she left, I walked up to Vice and wrapped my arms around his neck. This way my way of apologizing. I acted a complete ass earlier and I wanted to let him know I was sorry about that.

He held me by my waist and said, "You just don't get it yet, do you?"

I was confused, "Don't get what?"

He sat on the couch and I straddled him, "What would I need with a cubic zirconia, when I have a fucking diamond?"

I blushed, "Stop it."

He stared into my eyes and said, "I'm keeping it real with you, Storm. You don't have to worry about me out here fucking with anybody. Like I said, you're a fucking diamond ma. Flawless."

US AGAINST EVERYBODY: A DETROIT LOVE TALE 2

I laid my head on his chest, because staring into his eyes was becoming to be just too much. They were captivating. He rubbed my lower back, and whispered in my ear telling me I smelled good. I blushed again. I swear to God, this nigga made me feel like my shit didn't stink.

"I'm sorry Vice. I was totally out of line for earlier," I told him as I help him tighter.

"You did pop a nigga in the jaw. But it's cool, lil' mama, that feisty shit is sexy on the low."

I laughed and playfully examined his jaw. He pointed to an old scar and blamed it on me. We cracked up laughing. I was having so much fun with him that I forgot all about him reconnecting with his sister. Vice bringing it up, brought me back to reality.

He told me he seen some chick getting the shit beat out of her at the gas station that happened to be her. I didn't even bother asking him why he didn't call. That would've been selfish of me. I knew why he didn't call. He hadn't seen her in over fifteen damn years. When he told me where she was I couldn't believe it. It actually

223

broke my heart. I prayed he'd be able to forgive his mother, even though she did pass away years ago.

"He was molesting her, brown skin. And instead of reporting the shit, my mom's sent her away to boarding school," he chuckled. "What type of shit is that though?"

I rubbed his back, "I know it's fucked up—

"I'm on a mission. When I find the fuck nigga, I'm offing him. Off rip," said Vice through clinched teeth.

I didn't even say anything. What? Was I supposed to talk him out of it? How would that sound? I might not agree with house malicious he can be at times, but it's not my place to tell him not to do what he feels will be justice.

His phone rung. He checked it, and stuffed it back in his pockets.

"Who is that?"

"Jos—

"Why is she still calling?"

He rose his eyebrow at me and said, "I thought we just discussed you trusting me."

I jumped off of his lap, but he pulled me right back down.

"Storm," sternly said Vice.

US AGAINST EVERYBODY: A DETROIT LOVE TALE 2

"What," I snapped. I took a deep breath and changed my attitude, "Cubic zirconia?"

"Cubic fucking zirconia," he stood up and pulled me closer to him. "I'll add her to the block list. I can't change my number brown skin. You know why."

I almost asked him why he was speaking somewhat in code but I remembered. Laila didn't know what he did for a living. I understood why he wasn't open with her. In all actuality, he didn't know her. The only reason he looked out for her is because they share blood. She's his sister. But at the same time, he haven't seen her in years. They didn't know each other for real.

"Alright, nigga," I said to him with a smirk on my face. "You know how crazy I can get."

He smiled and mushed me in the head before walking off, "Yeah, I know. You ain't gon' like this shit, but brown skin I have shit to handle today."

I pulled my lips into my mouth and nodded as I walked behind him, "I figured." I sighed, "I guess I'll see you later?"

225

He looked at me over his shoulder as he slipped his Louboutin kicks on, "Fa sho. No lie, a nigga gone slide through… and then…" he sneakily smiled at me, "…I'ma slide through."

I laughed and threw a plastic cup at him, "You so fucking nasty."

Vice winked, "You love that shit though, lil mama." He opened his arms, "Give a nigga some love."

I smiled and hugged him. It felt good to be in his arms. I felt secure. Invincible even. Vice was something like my safe haven. So what if being with him means I can't have a father. Fuck a father, to be honest. Look at what he did just to tear me away from Vice. A man who's never hurt me like Mack did. That shit is supposed to be the other way around. My daddy is supposed to be my protector. Now a man I met less than a year ago is. And the only one to blame is Mack. He loss me. I didn't lose him. I did gain though. I gained a real nigga and from the looks of things, this union is going to last forever…if forever was possible.

Vice kissed me on my forehead, my cheeks, and then finally my lips. I grabbed the back of his neck and slipped some tongue in. He gripped my ass, and then pulled away.

"Got a nigga on some freak shit, lil mama," said Vice before rubbing his hard dick and rubbing it against my pussy. Relax, we're fully dressed.

US AGAINST EVERYBODY: A DETROIT LOVE TALE 2

I softly moaned and leaned my head against his, "We can get a room…"

He laughed and bit my lip, "Nah ma. I got shit to do. Check you out, tryna keep a nigga grounded."

We let go of each other and walked to the door. I poked my bottom lip out, pretending to pout.

"I'm horny though."

He smacked me on the ass, "You gone have to wait on this dick."

"What if I don't want to wait?"

His smile faded and he said, "You don't have a choice. Fuck is you saying?"

I laughed, "Relax fool. I didn't mean it like that."

He smiled, "I know," he coolly replied trying to play it off.

After saying our goodbye's I called Carla up immediately. There was no way in hell I was about to have her thinking my nigga was out here fucking over

227

me. It might seem petty to you but to me it's important. I put my man on a pedestal. I can't have her thinking he's anything less than perfect.

*

Driving, on my way home, I was so busy on the phone with Carla that I didn't notice the black van until it was too late. Had I been paying attention, I would've noticed it following since I left The Westin.

US AGAINST EVERYBODY: A DETROIT LOVE
TALE 2

[FIFTEEN]

Jai

"**W**ait, slow down," I yelled into the phone.

Carla called me all hysterical, saying something had happened to Storm. I had too much on my plate as is, and now it seemed like something terrible had happened.

I buckled my seatbelt and started my car.

"We were on the phone. I heard a loud crashing noise, and then the phone hung up," she was screaming crying. "You have to call Vice... her parents... somebody!"

I took a deep breath and closed my eyes, as to woosah. I was worried about Storm, that's for sure. But I was also worried about the shit I was into at the moment.

I was on some other shit, and what I just witnessed killed my whole entire fucking vibe.

"Okay, it probably was nothing. I'll call you back."

"It was something Jai! If it wasn—

I hung up on her crying ass. Why would I spend time on the phone listening to her whine when Storm could possibly be in danger? Of course I didn't have Vice's number, so I called momma instead. I didn't say anything about her being in danger. I casually asked if she's heard from Storm or not. She grew suspicious but I let her know everything was okay. Unfortunately she hadn't heard from Storm. I was worried then. Maybe something did happen. My heart rate increased as I thought of the possibility of her being hurt.

I sped in the direction of Vice's spot. I wasn't sure if I was even strong enough to be at a dope spot but desperate times call for desperate measures. Them niggas wouldn't sell me any coke if I begged for it though. Even with knowing that, the thought of asking still came to mind. I told myself to be strong.

I took a deep breath as I parked a few houses down. My hands began to sweat, and my mouth started to salivate. You know, how it does when you have a taste or urge for something. I shook my head and kept repeating to myself that I was here to get in touch with Vice. But what I found out earlier kept coming to mind. That shit alone made me want to take a hit.

US AGAINST EVERYBODY: A DETROIT LOVE TALE 2

I was on some ol stalking shit. Ryan wouldn't talk me so I decided to stalk his Facebook and Instagram. Thing is, he told me he didn't have any pages. I should've done research. Because if I would have, finding out he—

Tap, tap, tap.

I rolled my eyes and opened my car door, "What?"

"Fuck is you doing out here, Jai? You already know niggas ain't serving you up," said Reek's fine, chocolate, dread head ass.

"I'm clean, ass hole. I need Vice's number."

"For what?"

"I'm worried about Storm," I told him.

"Aight, bet. I can hit bro up right now," said Reek as he dialed Vice up.

I sat there impatiently tapping my fingernails against the steering wheel. My mind kept wandering right back to where I was headed before Carla called. I was about to go holla at Ryan's lying ass. As I was saying before

Reek rudely interrupted me, if I would've done my research on Ryan a long time ago, I would've known about –

"Bro said she left him about fifteen minutes ago. What's going on?"

I sucked my teeth and snatched his phone from his hands.

"Hey Vice,"

"Wassup, sis," said Vice making me feel all warm and loved inside.

"Carla said something happened when she was on the phone with Storm. She said it sounded like crashing and then the phone hung up,"

I waited for a response but never receive one. After holding the phone for a few seconds longer, I looked at it and discovered that Vice had hung up.

I sat dumbfounded before handing the phone back to Reek who told me that nine times out of ten Vice went looking for her. At that moment I realized that I was the only one not taking this serious. I was in denial. More so because I didn't want to even think about something potentially happening to Storm. I'd go crazy without her – she's my fucking backbone.

I immediately pulled off. I didn't even know where to look. Maybe Carla knows where Storm was coming

US AGAINST EVERYBODY: A DETROIT LOVE
TALE 2

from. I grabbed my phone and called her. She told me
was leaving The Westin in Southfield. After hanging up
with her, I drove as fast as I could to the nearest freeway.

As I sped down I-75, stress consumed me. My anger
was replaced with worry and freight. It was like God told
my ass there was bigger things to worry about than what I
was pissed about. Still, I couldn't help but think about
how Ryan played me. He was on my head about stripping
and shit, but he had a whole fucking child in Georgia.

Yes bitch, a secret baby. I mean, I never asked him if
he had kids but that's something you tell someone. I
decided that it'd be best if I popped up on his ass. He
didn't even know I knew. No wonder he told me he
didn't have Facebook or Instagram. While there were no
pictures of the little boy on his page, the bitch constantly
tagged him in photos. I was heated as hell when I found
out. The entire ride on i-75 and i696 west was spent
thinking about that shit. My thoughts went from Storm to
Ryan, Ryan to Storm. I didn't have to look for her until I
got off of 696 west, and onto 696 east where she was
driving. So I had time to call his ass since I literally just
got on 696 east.

I looked from the road, to my phone, as I scrolled through my contacts searching for Ryan's name. Finally, I found it and hit the dial button. See, popping up would've been more dramatic but since there was an emergency, plans had to be changed.

"Wassup," he answered sounding irritated.

I huffed, "Pssh, nigga what the fuck you irritated about?"

"Not now, Jai, please," said Ryan before sighing really loudly.

"Yes now! Why the fuck didn't you tell me you had a son!?"

Silence. I had to say hello to see if he was still there.

Ryan snorted and said, "Bye Jai."

I screamed into the phone, "Fuck you mean Bye!? Nigga we gone talk about this shit!"

I took the exit off the freeway with the phone pressed hard against my ear. I was pissed off. So pissed that tears were falling from my eyes. This sucka ass crying shit ain't even me!

"There's nothing to talk about," he told me matter-of-factly.

"Ryan, what are you saying!?"

US AGAINST EVERYBODY: A DETROIT LOVE TALE 2

He sighed, "I'm busy. Too busy to be entertaining this bull shit. Don't call me anymore, aight shawty? A nigga ain't gotta explain shit to you or anybody else! Matta fact, I'm blocking you bitch!"

When he hung up I stared at the phone. So long that I almost hit the back of someone's car. I was too upset to drive, so I pulled over on the side of the road. I sat there boohooing. I was in my feelings! Why was he acting like that? I didn't do a damn thing to him for him to snap on me like he did. That's typical nigga shit though! Get caught up and deflect. Fuck Ryan! Disrespectful, ugly ass nigga.

I wiped my tears and blew my nose on a Kleenex. It was time for me to go. Time for me to put the feelings I have for him away. Fuck his ugly ass. I was the best thing to happen to the fuck nigga! I was probably only dickmatized. No way in hell I could really be in love with someone as butt ugly as him! The dick good as fuck, that's all it probably is!

I shifted the car in drive and made a loop to hop on 696 east, where Storm was driving. But the traffic was unmoving. I pulled onto the freeway as best as I could.

Something was holding traffic up. And I couldn't see what. I rolled my window down and tapped my horn to grab the driver in front of me attention.

He stuck his head out of the window and yelled, "I know you see all of these cars backed up! I can't move, geniu—

"Keep calm and watch ya mouth, alright," I said pointing my finger at him, "I just want to know if you know what the hold-up is."

"Oh my bad sexy," I rolled my eyes and he continued, "It was on the radio. Something happened. A young woman was involved in a hit and run. Crazy shit is, they kidnapped her."

[SIXTEEN]

Vice

I didn't give a fuck. Once I made it on the freeway and seen all the cars backed up, I hopped out and ran to the scene. They tried to keep me back, and they did a good job at it. Storm's car sat in the middle of the freeway, smashed up. The cops didn't want to give me any information. Even after I lied and told them pussy niggas the victim was my fiancé. They didn't give a fuck but the people in traffic did. The ones who seen and heard everything. They gave me some valuable information. Sent me right on my fucking way.

Now, I sat in the whip with Dawson, chiefing from a blunt full of the best loud in the city. Of course it was the best; it's my shit. I picked cuz up as soon as I left the scene. I had to. It was only right. Reek was busy on the block, making sure shit moved swiftly.

I took a pull from the blunt, and looked at the fiery red tip as smoke slowly escaped my mouth. Before I picked cuz up, I hit the liquor store. Chugged a whole pint of Ciroc, straight no chase. I was fucked up out here. My diamond. My fucking diamond was gone. All because of a stupid ass fuck nigga.

I pulled off in the direction of the spot on Riopelle, where Reek was working. I couldn't believe a nigga I put on, and looked out for on some one hundred shit was responsible for this shit. I let my conscious cloud my better judgement. Niggas always want the number one spot. Why come for my lil' mama? Brown skin had nothing to do with this shit. I didn't want her involved in this life! Niggas didn't even know about her. Just my two trusted soldiers. Reek and Dawson. Can you believe the audacity?

"Where we going cuz," asked Dawson looking out of the window.

"Riopelle. Gotta holla at Reek about something."

He looked at me and said, "What it is? You found the black van?"

I chuckled and ignored him as I approached seven mile. He repeated his question and I said nothing. I turned the music up and handed the blunt to him. When he

US AGAINST EVERYBODY: A DETROIT LOVE TALE 2

reached for it I looked at his hand, then I jammed the blunt in his eye, and smashed his head against the dashboard.

Never did I suspect my blood. My fucking cousin. The whole mothafuckin time, worried about Reek being a fucking snake. Pulling burners on bro and shit. And for nothing.

While I was standing at the accident scene, begging for information, someone in traffic called me over. I walked up to her car and she told me she heard and seen everything since the accident was literally a few feet away from her. She was behind the black van.

"The young woman was a fighter. I tell you that," she shook her head with tears falling from her eyes, *"Two men approached her car after they hit her. As soon as they snatched her door open she yelled 'Dawson! What the fuck!?' She didn't stop screaming his name saying how Vice was going to fuck him up as she kicked and fought trying to get away from them. But the bigger guy, who I'm assuming was Dawson knocked her out cold. He was pissed because the little lady spit in his face and bit him. Right on his hand."*

So when Dawson reached for my blunt and I noticed teeth marks in his hand that was all the confirmation I needed. I made a right on Riopelle, just as Dawson was regaining cautiousness. He looked at me with his one good eye, as he screamed at the top of his lungs. I turned the stereo up louder as I parked in front of the spot. Reek came running down immediately. I had already wired bro up with the info.

He hopped in the backseat and I peeled off. Like I said before, I'm not the torturing type. But this shit chea, is the ultimate betrayal.

I turned the music down and calmly told Dawson to shut the fuck up. He didn't. But when I put fire to the blunt and pointed it at him, he did.

"So I'm going to ask you a few questions, *cuz*," I said, adding extra emphasizes on cuz.

He cried, "What nigga?! Fuck!"

I laughed, "You mad huh? Keep calm, *fam*, if you make it through this you'll be able to wear a cold ass eye patch." I looked at Reek through the rearview and said, "But we all know this nigga ain't making it, right?"

Reek shook his head and said, "You'a s fucking animal, brodie."

"Man what the fuck is this about," yelled Dawson.

US AGAINST EVERYBODY: A DETROIT LOVE
TALE 2

I burned him in the face with the blunt and said, "Stop raising yo voice in my fucking car, pussy!"

He squirmed and cried, "What…what's up cuz? We fam—

"You right, we're family! Which is why this shit hurt so bad nigga! Dawg, where my bitch at?!"

Dawson fell silent and looked out the window, his hand covering the other eye. I stomped down on the brakes and pulled the glock from under my seat and pressed it to the back of his head.

"Come on dawg, let a nigga have a little fun for once! I'm not trying to end things this way," I told him.

He kept his eyes on whatever he was looking at outside the window, "I didn't mean for shit to get this bad. You know how I feel about loyalty, man. But I couldn't sit back and wa—

"Nigga, spare me the bullshit. Just tell me where my bitch at."

"You gone let me walk if I do so?"

241

I smirked and shook my head, "Yeah, cuz, I'ma let you walk."

He tensed up and said, "No the fuc—

I pressed the gun harder against his skull, "Nigga I said I was! You tryna call me a liar?!"

"Aight, aight, cuz! She...she's at Joslyn's spot."

I sat there confused for a minute. Fuck he mean she's at Joslyn's spot. Fuck he mean dawg? Didn't I tell that bitch that if I have any more problems out of her I'm snatching the life right up out of her? I was shocked. So fucking shocked that a nigga was cracking up laughing. There wasn't anything funny though. I was full of rage. So much rage that I pulled the trigger.

Reek yelled, "What the fuck brodie," as he looked around making sure hook wasn't near.

I didn't give a fuck. He realized just how much I didn't care when I pulled off with Dawson's dead body sitting there. Busted window, brain matter, and blood all over my face.

Reek sat behind me and shook my shoulders from the backseat. He was trying to pull me to reality. Trying to tell me I was being stupid sloppy but I didn't care. I pressed my feet down on the gas pedal, heading to Joslyn's spot. Thing is, she stayed down town. And down town is always flooded with hook.

US AGAINST EVERYBODY: A DETROIT LOVE TALE 2

"Vice! Nigga! You gotta pull this bitch over bro! You tryna get us thrown under the jail yo!"

I blinked my eyes repeatedly before finally slowing the car down from seventy, to thirty. I glanced at Dawson and the thought of me having to tell my auntie her son was killed crossed my mind. I felt no remorse from killing him but I did have ill feelings about giving the news to my aunt.

"What we gone do," I asked as I stared at Reek threw the rearview.

He was silent. Mainly because I've never came at him not knowing what to do. I was lost at the moment. I couldn't think straight and that was because I was imagining what could possibly be going down at Joslyn's spot. How she could be doing my baby was killing me. Brown skin was caught up in all of this shit because of me. I'll never be able to forgive myself if that stupid bitch Joslyn does something like... man I can't even bring myself to say what I'm thinking.

I regretted not offing that emotional bitch when I had the chance. I just didn't think she would be so fucking stupid to do something like this. Now that I think about it,

243

the bitch hit my line earlier. What the fuck could she had possibly wanted? I needed to hurry up and get there before it's too late. I can't even think of how I'd feel if I walked in on some bull shit. In such a short period of time, Storm and I had become one. And if I loss shorty, I'll be losing a piece of me too.

Finally, Reek spoke.

"Pull this bitch in the alley over there," he pointed.

I made a quick left and pulled into the alley, praying to God no one saw us. Dawson's limp body fell against me, and I roughly pushed him off of me. I shifted the car in park and asked Reek what was next.

"Push the nigga out, bro," said Reek.

I looked at him and laughed, "Bet."

I leaned over and opened the door, then pushed Dawson. I didn't even look down at him before I closed the door back and drove away. He was nothing to me. The respect and love I had for him went away once I found out he was behind the shit.

"Swing back around the way. Put this bitch in the garage until we can take it to the chop shop," said Reek, "We can ride in my whip."

I just nodded and kept my eyes on the road. The blood and brain matter was starting to irritate my skin, so I rubbed it away. I placed my hands back on the steering

US AGAINST EVERYBODY: A DETROIT LOVE TALE 2

wheel and looked down at the stuff that transferred from my face to my hand. I smirked, fuck nigga. What? Nigga thought he was exempt because we shared the same blood? I told lil' mama! I'll cause havoc out to this bitch. And I meant on anybody!

What had me a little vexed was why? Why did Dawson bitch up and try to play me? I cursed myself for not getting more information before I offed him. But fuck it! Niggas a goner. That's all that really matters. I couldn't give a fuck less about why.

I drove into the garage at the spot and cut the engine off, before lowering the garage door. I looked in my passenger seat and instantly became pissed. The Audi is my favorite car. Now I'll have to get my baby chopped up. All because a bitch nigga couldn't keep it G!

I hopped out the whip, and Reek did too. He had his phone glued to his ear, talking to the chop shop guy. I started to walk out of the garage, but he held me back. I looked at him like he lost his mind and he motioned at my face. I had Dawson all over me. I yanked away from Reek and stuck my key in the trunk lock. I had all type of shit in here. What was going on had me off my game a lil bit.

I stripped of everything but my draws, and threw the clothes in a little pile in a corner. I grabbed a few wet wipes out of a canister and proceeded to wipe my face and body down. I tossed the wipes in the corner and put a black t-shirt over my head. I slid on a pair of Nike basketball shorts, although it's only about thirty degrees out. That's all I had. I looked down at my shoes and brains were even on them. Fuck! I kicked my Loubti's off and tossed them in the pile, and put on a pair of Gucci flip flops.

I grabbed the can of gasoline out and proceeded to close the trunk. Again, Reek stopped me and shook his head.

When he got off the phone he said, "I know how bad you wanna get to Storm, but we gotta clean the shit up bro."

He looked into the trunk, grabbed some bleach wipes and two rain ponchos.

He handed me a poncho and I put it on over my head. This shit had me so out of my mind, I was about to leave the murder scene dirty. I had to get my head screwed on straight. I grabbed some bleach wipes from Reek and we both walked over to the passenger side, where Dawson took his last breath.

US AGAINST EVERYBODY: A DETROIT LOVE TALE 2

I opened the door and we began to clean everything up. Reek kept trying to make small talk but I wasn't in the mood to rap. All I kept thinking about was getting to my lil' mama pronto. Reek knew I was losing it, so he was doing his best at keeping shit afloat. I appreciated the fuck out of bro for that. He's a trill ass nigga. I low key regret even pulling the burner on him on so many occasions.

After we finished cleaning up, we wiped the car down and got rid of everything I had in it. By time we were finished, the duffle bag I had in the back was full to capacity. I poured gasoline on the clothes, and wipes we used to clean up with and lit a match. Once that burned down to ashes, I swept it up and tossed them in the trashcan.

Finally, we were in Reek's whip, heading to Joslyn's crib. Bro sat there steady trying to talk to me and make light of the situation. He could see the fire in my eyes. He was trying to calm me but it wasn't working. I saw Reek's lips moving but I didn't hear a thing he said.

All I kept thinking of is the last time I held her. The kiss we shared, and how bad I wanted to fuck her. I should've. I wish I fucking would've.

"Her spot right there," I told Reek when we finally made it down town.

My heart raced with fear and excitement all at once.

Reek parked down from her crib and I hopped out before he even came to a complete stop.

Before I made it to Joslyn's crib though, I stopped dead in my tracks. How did I not notice the three squad cars and ambulance parked out front before we parked? My palms began to sweat, and my mouth got dry.

"Fuck, bro," said Reek as paramedics walked out of Joslyn's crib with a body on the stretcher with a sheet thrown over it.

I took off running. A nigga would've thought I ran track if they witnessed how fast I was running. Before I could make it to them, a cop stopped me.

"I'm sorry son, you can't go—

"Who the fuck is that yo? Who's body is...."

My voice trailed off as I witnessed the cops walking someone out of the house handcuffed. I squinted my eyes, trying to get a good look at the person. They were covered in blood. When she walked by me, our eyes met.

US AGAINST EVERYBODY: A DETROIT LOVE TALE 2

I tried to get at her, and she tried to get at me. I tried my best, as did she. We couldn't help it. We were attracting to one another. Like a negative, to a fucking positive. The cop held me back as best as he could, but I eventually got away. But it was too late. Brown skin was already in the back of the squad car. I looked inside at her. She looked back at me. Instead of crying, like she was when they walked her to the car, she was smiling.

What the fuck happened?

-To be continued-

SNEAK PEEK

-Untitled-

"Stay here. I'll be back," said Justice bossing me around as usual.

I was growing tired of this bitch but I only stayed around because I needed her for the moment. I played like a broke nigga who was only dealing with a cheating bitch because she took care of me. Yeah, I might seem like less than a man to you but believe me, I know what I'm doing. I let her think she had me on lock. Nah, never. I sit here watching her bad ass kids because this is what I have to do for now. Pretty soon this bitch and this fucked up situation will only be a memory.

I paused NBA 2k16 and looked up at her. She was dressed provocatively and had on entirely too much makeup. I didn't tell her that though. I lied and told her she looked good. Justice leaned over and kissed me on the forehead. I almost threw up at the smell of her knock off Chanel perfume.

I sat the Xbox One controller on the coffee table and pulled her down for a hug. I played my role well. I couldn't care less about this thot bitch.

US AGAINST EVERYBODY: A DETROIT LOVE
TALE 2

"Where else would I be besides here, baby?" I
kissed her on the cheek, "Make our money. I'll see you
later."

I was behaving like a broke bum nigga but I'm far
from one. Everything I did had motive. Everything I
did was for a reason. Justice was nothing but an
opportunity for a quick come up. I had this blueprint
written out months before I even approached her.

"You got it daddy," said Justice before getting up
and kissing her kids goodbye in the mouth with lips
she just sucked my dick with.

I pressed play on the game and passed her
youngest son, Kevin, the other controller. I chuckled
watching him press buttons like he was actually
playing. I had not a care in the world for Justice but I
did love her four kids like nieces and nephews I never
had. I took better car of them than she did. I bathed
and fed them while she was out shaking her
ridiculously fat ass at King of Diamonds every night.

Still over there thinking I'm a bum ass nigga right?
Get those crazy thoughts up out your mental. I'm far

from a broke dude. I have money, I have cribs, and I have a numerous amount of whips. I'm responsible for over half of the coke, weed, lean, and molly on the streets of Detroit Michigan but not too many people knew that. I kept a low profile.

What I was doing could potentially keep me set for a few years. Justice, named after her late kingpin father, was sitting on a fortune and I was impatiently waiting for her to slip up.

"Julien ," said Natalie, the oldest and my favorite of the bunch.

I paused the game, "Wassup little mama?"

"There's blood in my panties," replied Natalie nervously.

I sat there in shock. She's twelve, and just started her period while her mom's out popping her pussy for a buck. I didn't know what to do. I didn't say anything for at least three minutes before she repeated herself. I didn't know what the fuck to do.

"Hol up, let me call yo moms."

I just met these kids four months ago. Taking care of shit like this is a mother's responsibility. Hell, I'm still a stranger to them. Thank God I'm not a twisted mothafucka because if I was Justice sure wouldn't know. Got me up in here with these kids like she really

US AGAINST EVERYBODY: A DETROIT LOVE
TALE 2

know me. I could be going upside these lil niggas
heads. But I have love for kids and wouldn't harm one
if my life depended on it.

I pulled my Galaxy Note 4 from my pocket and
called her moms. She didn't answer and after the
fourth attempt I said fuck it. Bitch was too busy to
answer. It could've been an emergency. I swear she
didn't care about these kids.

I sighed and stood up, "Ay, she didn't answer." I
rubbed my bald head then asked, "Yo moms ain't got
no pads in the bathroom?"

"Pads? For what?" asked Natalie not knowing
anything about a damn period.

"You started your period, lil mama," I replied
shaking my head, "Yo moms supposed to talk to you
about this."

Still she was confused. I walked to the bathroom
and looked in the medicine cabinet for pads. All
Justice had were tampons. I wasn't about to have this
little girl stick that shit in her lil' virgin vagina.
Realizing that I would have to go out and get pads

253

pissed me off even more but I wouldn't show the kids my anger. Especially not Natalie who had not a clue of what was going on.

I put the other kids to bed and told Natalie to hop in the tub while I ran out and got pads. She nodded and embarrassingly walked away. I called Justice a few more times before heading out. I didn't even know what the fuck to get. Back when I was a little nigga moms use to send me to the store for pads but that was years ago and I didn't know what was out now.

I threw my hoodie on and headed to the liquor store on the corner. It was a chilly spring night but the block was hot. I was on seven mile and Van Dyke – the hood for sure. I never left the crib without a burner. Niggas over here didn't know me but they used my product. I was a low-key type of cat. I didn't like attention nor the drama and fame that came with it. I liked the fact that niggas didn't know me.

I had been in this drug game for over five years, and had racked in over a million dollars but you'd never be able to tell by the way I carried myself. Twenty-eight year old owner of six houses on the west side of Detroit. The money stayed flowing in but I didn't waste my money on shit like True Religion, Gucci belts, Ray Bands, or any other designer bullshit out here. I invested and was cool with throwing on a

US AGAINST EVERYBODY: A DETROIT LOVE TALE 2

pair of Levi's, some Nikes – or possibly some J's – and a v-neck shirt.

I walked in the liquor store and removed my hood. Niggas crowded the counter, rowdy asking for a pint of Ciroc. A pint of liquor for seven niggas. Cats were broke and I found that shit humorous. Broke ass niggas trying to keep up with the times. A group of attractive women entered the store as I was in the aisle looking for the pads. Of course the thirst got real and those same broke niggas hounded them. Every last one of the females threw shade.

A dark skinned pretty chick walked down the aisle and I stopped her.

"Sorry to bother you, but my lil' sis just started her period," I said making a puppy dog face, "and a brotha don't know what the hell I'm looking for."

She giggled and handed me a pack of Always with wings. I thanked her and she winked then walked away. I watched her phat ass jiggle in her leggings as she sashayed down the aisle . I wanted to get to know her but Natalie was at the crib waiting on these so I simply paid for the pads and walked out of the store.

"Hey!" yelled somebody as I was headed back to Justice's shit.

I turned around and recognized shorty from the liquor store with her head out the passenger side window flagging me down. I pointed to myself to make sure she wanted me and she nodded. I walked over to the whip, and noticed the same dusty ass niggas were posted outside of the store watching.

I asked her what was up and she told me she wanted to talk to me later. She handed me her iPhone 6 and told me to put my number in there. I didn't know what it was about me that interested her. I was dressed down as usual but let's not get it twisted, I'm a handsome dude. I stood at a towering 6'6 muscle bond, caramel skin with a goatee and a bald head.

I guess she found me attractive. The bums stood there sour as fuck, making sly remarks.

"Broke ass nigga," mumbled one of them.

After finishing my small convo with 'dark skin' I approached the group of niggas and said, "Don't be dumb trying to impress bitches and get fucked up." I mean mugged them and patted my waist.

US AGAINST EVERYBODY: A DETROIT LOVE TALE 2

No one budged and I walked away without an ounce of fear in me.

-Coming 2016-

Also On Sale by Miss Candice

Us Against Everybody

If Not For Love Series - Books 1-4

Intoxicated: Blinded by Love Series - Books 1-3

US AGAINST EVERYBODY: A DETROIT LOVE TALE 2

Join our mailing list to get a notification when Leo Sullivan Presents has another release!

Text LEOSULLIVAN to 22828

to join!

To submit a manuscript for our review, email us at leosullivanpresents@gmail.com

CPSIA information can be obtained
at www.ICGtesting.com
Printed in the USA
LVOW04s1738021216
515533LV00009B/572/P